Pure

Nara Vidal

Translated by Nathalia Baroni Faula

First published in 2025 by Printim Editions

Printed and bound by TJ Books 2025

ISBN 979-8-9874792-1-6

Copyright © Printim Editions 2025

The right of Nara Vidal to be identified as the owner of this work has been asserted by her in accordance with the Copyright, Designs and Patents Act 1988

All rights reserved. No part of this publication may be reproduced, stored in a retrieval system, or transmitted, in any form, or by any means (electronic, mechanical, photocopying, recording or otherwise) without the permission of the publisher.

Translated from Portuguese into English by Nathalia Baroni Faula

First Edition

Originally published as *Puro* (2023) by Editoria Todavia, São Paulo, Brazil

228 Park Avenue S.
New York, NY 10003
www.printimeditions.com

For Monique and Sâmia

Prelude

We, therefore, grant Your Excellency, the King of Portugal and Spain, through this document, with our apostolic authority, total and free permission to invade, hunt, capture, and subjugate pagans or any other non-believer and enemy of Christ, whoever they may be, as well as their kingdoms, counties, duchies, principalities, and other properties, in order to reduce them to perpetual servitude.
Dum diversas, 1452

Article 138 — It is the duty of the Union, the states, and the municipalities:
- to encourage eugenic education;
- to take care of mental hygiene and promote the fight against social poisons.

Constitution of the United States of Brazil, 1934

God, Homeland, and Family
    slogan of the Brazilian Integralist Action, 1930s

God, Homeland, Race, and Family
    slogan of the Brazilian Black Front, 1930s

There are three old women living in a large, and also old house.

In this big house, there is a boy of about fifteen years old.

Lázaro is neither son nor grandson of any of them. He is tutored at home. Dália teaches him religion and piano. Lobélia teaches him languages. Alpínia teaches cooking and basic anatomy. The radio is always loud so the old women can listen to music, and, as the children in the town say, to drown out the voices from the attic.

The town is called Santa Graça — a reference to virtue and cleanliness in the national territory. In the future, there would be no more black children or sick people there.

Ícaro crosses the ocean
Brazil, 1930s

LÁZARO SHOUTS:
Wash your hands, Íris, scrub them well. Wash them properly to see if the black comes off.

ÍRIS THINKS:
Liar boy. Lázaro says he comes from Germany, but old Alpínia says the boy isn't very trustworthy, and his origins are more local and precise: Três Vendas, a rural area of Santa Graça. His mother, whom no one knew, left the child on the street. Once, Dália and Lobélia were passing through the village to buy quince from Fazenda Bela Vista and came across a bundle of rags inside a basket. It was a very white boy. They looked around. The air was clear. Dry. No one. The afternoon had settled down. No one anywhere under the intense, orange heat. The two of them sat on the chapel steps and waited almost the whole afternoon for someone to call for the boy. That was how Lázaro was born. Born from no one wanting him.

He was as white as a cloud, very rare to find such a pure child, without a father or mother. What was abundant were the black children with no family. There were plenty of those. They roamed in packs, begging for food scraps and water at the houses of Santa Graça's wealthy families. That's how I grew up, that's how many children from Mata Cavalo grew up, and that's how my Joaquim would have grown up if he had survived.

One Monday, after the boy Ícaro came back from school, he hung onto the balcony of his mother's room and saw four or five boys stopping by the big house. People of my kind: ragged clothes in the orange hue of beaten earth. They asked for a glass of water. Here at Ícaro's house, I can't open the door for them, Ícaro's grandmother won't let me. When they see me through the gate, they shout my name, asking me to get them some leftover bread. If I go, Dona Rosa will send me away. Ícaro and the little black boys can't even talk. Dona Rosa and the boy's mother, Dona Ondina, taught him that black children went into other people's houses to steal. They were different from the gypsies who entered to read our palms and tell us about the future; they stole, and we didn't even notice. The dark-skinned boys would, if necessary, hit others and take things bought with so much sacrifice. Dona Rosa also said they were lazy because if white people studied and worked to earn life's comforts, why didn't black people do the same?

I am healthy, and I thank the Lord every night. I also wish to kill Dona Rosa. Father Arcanjo taught me to pray to God and Jesus. He is a holy man; he also taught me not to be sad about serving others. Everything is God's will, and He knows what He is doing. The kingdom of heaven belongs to me. Father Arcanjo reminded me of the good life I had. My grandmothers were certainly slaves, and, thank God, things have improved a lot.

I stepped away from the window so the boys wouldn't see me, then peeked when they clapped and rang the doorbell of the three witches. Ícaro was there, watching them. Poor thing, he just wanted to play.

Lobélia opened the door. She gestured for them to wait on the porch, and I saw when she called someone from inside the house. Dália went to the porch, gave them gentle pats on the head, and they opened their mouths, showing their teeth, but they weren't smiling. Alpínia arrived with water, biscuits, and a towel, which Dália used to wipe her hands after touching the children. She told them to come back the next day at the same time to get some bread. The boys stepped down from the porch that led to the street. They seemed happy. Their dirty hands clutched the black caramels they had received, the ones with a burnt taste that stuck to your teeth. One of the little black boys saw Ícaro. He smiled with all his teeth, the same ones he had just shown the old ladies from the big house. Ícaro got scared, not of the boy, but that his grandmother would see him smiling at the kid. He hid behind the curtain. I felt a sharp pain near my right ear. I looked at the ground. I looked at the black boy. He smiled again, waved, and left. I picked up the caramel he had thrown to Ícaro from the polished wooden floor.

Tuesday, Wednesday and Thursday the same thing happened. The boys from Mata Cavalo knocked on the door of the big house and either Alpínia or Lobélia would give them stale bread and water. Dália tapped them lightly on their heads, filled their filthy hands with caramels and they left. The same boy who threw Ícaro the candy also threw several more until Friday came, which was the last time I saw Ester's boy.

ÍCARO THINKS:
Íris washes the dishes, washes the clothes,
washes the floor and her hand stays black.

She scrubs the laundry in the washbasin, uses bleach on the floor of the veranda. It's no use: her hand is always black.

I saw that the boy with the caramels and four others clapped at the door of the big house, and this time they went in. It was almost 7 o'clock in the evening, and the smell of soup coming from there was a sign that the boys had been invited to sit at the table and eat like proper people. Maybe a chunk of fresh bread to go with the corn cream I could smell from the veranda in my mother's room.

I watched from the window until eight o'clock, when my mother shouted that dinner was ready. From seven to eight, there was no sign of them. They must have been stuffing themselves with real food.

I had a hard time falling asleep. The street had been silent for hours, and I still couldn't drift off. I kept thinking about the boy with the caramel; a black boy couldn't be my friend. Grandma would never allow it. Neither would Mom or Dad. During the week, we played by tossing a caramel back and forth—him over there, me over here. I looked under the curtain, scanned the whole orange-toned wooden floor, but I didn't find anything.

The ducks at the big house made a racket, and it was already late. They screamed as if someone were robbing the house. Nothing ever happened in Santa Graça, though. It was just the dog, either angry or hungry. Loud barking that went on for almost half an hour. When the animal finally stopped barking, I fell asleep.

LÁZARO SAYS:
Íris washes dishes, washes clothes, washes the floor, and her hand is still black. She scrubs the laundry in the washbasin, bleach on the veranda floor. It's no use: her hand is black and dirty.

My birth mother was German. She gave me away because she didn't have a husband. Father Arcanjo asked the three old women to look after me and raise me. My blood is pure, just look at me. I don't want to play with Ícaro because he's a retard.

DONA ROSA ORDERS:
Go play with Lázaro, Ícaro. He's a good boy. Íris can't look after you. She has to clean the house, wash the bathrooms—she gets all dirty. Don't touch her, son. God made everyone in different colors

so we could understand each person's role. And we're not going to argue with God. Imagine that!

OLAVO EXPLAINS:

I'm crazy about my son. Ícaro is a good boy, but he has many limitations. Something genetic that we can't explain. Ondina and I do everything for this boy, and we want him to have a normal life. He goes to school. He's very loved by the other students. I don't know if they feel sorry for him, with those wobbly legs he has, poor thing. But the normal kids love Ícaro. You can tell just by looking at his little face. God is the Almighty Father, and He gave us this boy to take care of. We spend a lot on Ícaro, the medicines are expensive, but they're worth every penny to see him doing better. Ondina is an excellent wife. I hit the jackpot. We were blessed with Ícaro.

OLAVO THINKS:

How this child drools, stumbles, it embarrasses me. Fly, Ícaro, fly.

ÍCARO THINKS:

Every Saturday, at noon, the whole street hears Lázaro's piano lessons. He combines piano with singing, and the lesson lasts up to an hour and a half. It's also when the dog goes crazy. Piano, barking, and singing fill the street. From my room, I can feel the ground shaking. The clock strikes one-thirty, and the silence returns to the house. The loud sounds coming from that big house on Saturdays often bother me. When it gets hard to bear all that noise, I bang my head against the wall to see if all that noise will leave me.

With no school to go to that day, I spent the whole time by the window, trying to see the caramel boys. Nothing. They must have left the big house while I was having dinner. We missed each other. Íris didn't see when they left either. They might have passed by after six. Surely, they'd feel hungry and thirsty and ring the doorbells until someone gave them some leftover food. The boy with the shiny black eyes would look for me and throw another caramel on the floor of my mother's room for us to play with. But he didn't come, neither at six, nor at seven, nor at any time.

From the big house came a strong smell of food. They were cooking the Sunday meal. The three sisters cooked together. From the back room of my house, I could see a corner of their wood stove. Huge pots. The constant fire, an endless process of food, cutlery, and herbs collected from the garden. The kitchen was dark, old. Every Sunday, they made seasoned, aromatic meats, top cuts, just like Alpínia used to say when she saw me in the back window, watching their lives.

ONDINA THINKS:

Every Sunday, before lunch, the three women from the big house go to Mass. I also go. Olavo and Mom accompany me. We take Ícaro because my boy really needs prayers. Our Lady of Miracles will intercede and give him the strong legs he deserves, a clear and pure speech, the right mind, poor thing. We share the bread, which is the body of Christ, and swallow the soggy cake that becomes the host after the brief prayer. God forgive me, but that makes my stomach turn ever since catechism.

The old women and the boy Lázaro go. Then, they return with Father Arcanjo, who lunches at the big house every Sunday, without fail.

The whole Sunday passes, and Father Arcanjo leaves the big house at four in the afternoon. He carries a bag and a lunchbox. The old women pamper the Father as much as they can. They are very devout and maintain a close friendship with him. From time to time, Father Arcanjo takes Lázaro with him to the church. When it happens that I'm on the veranda and see the two of them leave, the Father explains that Lázaro takes Latin lessons with him on Sunday afternoons, during his time off from prayers.

ONDINA COMMENTS:
Latin lessons... Sure...

ÍRIS MAKES
Olavo coffee.

OLAVO WATCHES
Íris wash the soapy spoon up and down, up and down.

ÍCARO THINKS:
That Sunday, I waited once again for the boys from the street to come to the big house and ask for food, but they didn't. My parents kept insisting that I play with that weird Lázaro. He used to say that he was a doctor and would cut bugs in half. He sewed and glued spider legs onto ant bodies. He also had a collection of bones that he'd find underground. Lobélia said that before they bought the land where the big house was built, it had been a dog

cemetery. But that was just a story to scare children. What was under the ground were really people, buried many years ago, turning into fertilizer and legend. Lázaro found bones and built skeletons of imaginary beings. Monsters that he saw.

At night, around six, the dog barked with all its might. The radio was at full volume because of the deaf old women. An hour later, silence. The stillness of the early Sunday night was broken by the creaking of the iron gate, covered in mud and rust. Father Arcanjo was bringing Lázaro back. He praised the boy's progress in Latin and mentioned that Lázaro had already taken a bath. The boy had enjoyed eating some *doce de leite*[1] and gotten messier than was acceptable for a boy his size. The holy father then suggested that he clean up at the parish house before going home. Without further conversation, Alpínia bid the Father farewell, and he climbed up the hill, holding his cassock to avoid tripping, head down, always humble.

I went to sleep without forgetting the caramel boy. The boy who, it seemed, was missing.

---

1. *Doce de leite* is a popular confection in Brazil, and especially produced in Minas Gerais. It is made by cooking milk and sugar for several hours until reaching a gooey texture.

LÁZARO SAYS:

I don't want to play with you, you retarded Ícaro. Get away from the window!

When I grow up, I'm going to be mayor. I'll rule the whole town. Crazy people like you will go to Fazenda Horizontina. I'm going to start a house for the insane. The town will be nice and clean. Where's your black maid? When God made man, the good ones got in line and bathed in the lake of purity. I was the first in line. Íris didn't make it in time and only washed the palm of her hand and the sole of her foot. That's why she's black and dirty.

You don't know how to take a joke, do you, you retarded Ícaro?

ÍRIS THINKS:

Santa Graça is a village like any other. It works just fine: post office, two primary schools, one secondary school, the bus station, the shopping street with grocery stores, butcher shops, a bakery, stationery store, a bank, two bars, a library. It has notable residents: Father Arcanjo, the mayor, Mr. Olavo, Dr. Lírio, and others whose professions are not really known. Jão da Lavagem has a first and last name, but he's only known by the trash he carries in his wheelbarrow.

He pulls the cart up and down, knocking on doors, asking if there's any *lavagem*.[2] The residents separate leftover food and fat into large cans, which Jão collects every afternoon at five. That *lavagem* is used to feed his pigs, which turn into sausages—the most delicious sausages—from Getúlio's butcher shop in the village center.

Every now and then, my Jão da Lavagem, who isn't mine, stops at the big house's door, where Dália brings heavy cans of fat. Fat so thick it can't be thrown away at the back of the yard. I'm the one who collects it every week. It even gives me back pain, how heavy the fat is. Jão is thankful for the impressive thickness of the fat. The pigs love it. It's top-quality stuff for the animals. It's hard to see the green eyes of my Jão, who is no longer mine.

ÍCARO THINKS:

The regular *lavagem* of the houses in Santa Graça doesn't compare to the one at the big old house. Íris works here and also for the neighbors. Íris collects the buckets, and her back curves from the weight. The kids at school say that the thick fat from the big house is made from magical potions of leftover food from the cauldron of the three witches. The three sisters cook almost all the time. From the edge of my window, I can see the fire that's never put out, the pots always high and deep, cooking

---

2. *Lavagem* refers to the leftover meat collected from the houses and used to feed the pigs.

something that never gets ready, like a stew
made from animal bones and feet.

> **LÁZARO SAYS:**
> The *lavagem* from the other houses in Santa Graça doesn't compare to that of my house. They say that the thick slop and fat are made from magical potions of leftover food from the pots of my mothers. The three of them cook all the time. A magical potion made from bone, ear, and feet.
>
> Ícaro, you're retarded and you drool. Íris is black and dirty. I'm white and pure.

ÍRIS THINKS:

It had been a month since I was watching the neighbor's gate, waiting to see the boys from the street, the ones from Mata Cavalo, knock on the door again. But they had already vanished. Ester was in distress because her son had disappeared with his friends, all kids from my street. Dona Rosa said that little black boys were always bothering good peoples' homes, asking for food, playing pranks, and disturbing others' work instead of looking for a job. I'm going to ask Father Arcanjo if I can confess. How I wish to kill Dona Rosa.

DONA ROSA ORDERS:
Íris, clean the bathroom again. It's not clean enough.

You have to scrub, my dear. Separate your utensils, okay? You left everything in the sink, and you won't know which ones are yours, and then you'll mix them with ours. Pay attention, my dear. Pay attention, please.

DONA ROSA THINKS
exactly what she says.

ÍCARO THINKS:
There was one day when I heard Grandma tell Mom that Íris was worried because the boys from her street, the children of her friends, had hit the road and gone to the neighboring town. That's when I understood that the boys from the street had fled. I felt jealous of them, that they could go to other towns in groups with their friends, eating caramels whenever they wanted and walking without tripping. I think Íris was sad because the mothers of the boys wanted to alert the police about their disappearance, but no one seemed to care. They said the little black boys would come back when they were hungry

or needed to change clothes because they were dirty, messy, and stinky. The mothers of the children, including two women who worked at the mayor's house, shouldn't worry. That was just kids being kids.

LÁZARO SAYS:
The little black boys will come back when they're hungry, Ícaro.

They'll come back filthy, messy, and even blacker. They'll come back dirty. And Íris, who scrubs and scrubs and still doesn't get any whiter—have you seen that?

The little black boys disappeared from Santa Graça because they went to the big city to sell drugs.

Ícaro, why do you drool so much? And at your age, you still haven't learned how to walk?

THE THREE SISTERS SAY:
The little black boys will come back when they miss home. That's how children are. When they're dirty and stinky, those little black boys will come back to bother us again, asking for candy. That's how children are. These little black boys, raised without

going to mass... Here's the result. It's not just our imagination, it's the truth. Do you think Lázaro would run away from home? That's what a neglected boy does.

DONA ROSA ASKS DONA ONDINA:
Does Olavo know what happened to those little black boys?

In Mata Cavalo, Íris said they're thinking about calling the radio, someone to report their disappearance. Do you know where those boys are, Ondina? What about Olavo?

OLAVO EXPLAINS:
Hey Ondina, tell your mother to mind her own business. That annoying old hag.

Since the news about the disappearance of the caramel boys spread from Mata Cavalo to the center of Santa Graça, those miserable women started keeping their little black boys at home. They say they're in danger, and some even claim they didn't go to the neighboring town at all; that they were kidnapped instead.

OLAVO THINKS:
Fly, Ícaro, fly.
Die, Ícaro.

Would you believe that, Ondina! Who would kidnap a black boy? If it were a child with blue eyes, blonde or brown hair, that would make sense, but who would want the black ones? Surely, they all ran away together. Some even say they went to the big city, where criminals recruit boys with no future like those boys.

ÍRIS PICKS UP
The trash from the ground.

OLAVO WATCHES
Íris on all fours.

ÍRIS THINKS:
Just to be safe, my friends started locking up the remaining children at home, keeping a close eye on them, and even with other kids around, it was dangerous to let them go out. The disappearance of the boys was sad for Mata Cavalo. In the town center, they said it was normal for the boys to disappear and that it was expected they would vanish. They didn't even seem to care about what might have happened to them. One thing was certain in the town: no one would ever kidnap little black boys. There was nothing to gain from that. Over in Mata Cavalo, they started holding a meeting every night with offerings to the deities, asking for help to find the boys.

ÍCARO THINKS:
I am thirteen years old and I go to school sometimes. My grandmother takes care of me while my parents work. I can't count past ten and I hear voices coming from under my bed. The ghost of my grandfather visits me at night when I can't sleep. When I was eight, I spent my birthday in a sanatorium. I don't remember, but my mother told me I went to spend a few days being observed because I tried to jump out of my window. I would have fallen into the big tank where the ducks and geese from the big house drink water. A thick, muddy liquid that smells all day long, but it's the path to cross the ocean. I hate having to go to school because, of course, they just laugh at me. A teacher always comes to keep me company because she feels sorry for me. I would rather be alone, but they won't let me. I like to stay at home, watch the neighbors, and look at that big house. There's always something strange about it that the whole town believes is haunted. There's a mystery on the second floor that no one knows. In all my years of life, I've never seen a window on the second floor open. They're always closed, no matter how sunny it gets. My father says they're closed not because of ghosts, but because pigeon

nests were made there, and the old women don't have money to fix the roof's ceiling. That's why they keep everything shut—the windows and the door that leads to the second floor through the living room stairs.

But the pigeons, if they exist, can't explain the screams of distress and the cries I hear from the second floor. I've heard them several times. Of course, I hear voices, and that's why they give me medicine. I see the ghost of my grandfather and no one believes me. I also don't beg them to believe me. I know I'm strange, I have no friends, and I like to get attention. At my age, the only thing I know how to do is drool. Walking – putting one foot in front of the other, that I can't do.

The only kids who want to play with me are the street boys. But I can't even touch them. Iris told me that Grandma, Mom, and Dad are disgusted by any hand that is black, but it is funny that no one complains about the food she makes, the beds she arranges, the clothes she washes and irons. When she gets like this, possessed, she goes to church and Father Arcanjo prays for her. Iris said that one day she'll take me to her house to play with the boys from Mata Cavalo. I dream of that day, but it never comes. I don't want to play with Lázaro. Yesterday I saw when he cut off a frog's legs and glued a chicken bone on each side. I'm afraid of Lázaro, but I don't want him to know.

ÍRIS THINKS:

Poor Ícaro. Sick boy in the head, the best thing he can do is stare at the big house. The good thing about being crazy is that most of the time no one bothers you. Ícaro watches the house day and night, always from his bedroom window, his mom's bedroom balcony, or the living room window. He constantly spies on the dirty water tank for the ducks. It shines with a beautiful rainbow at lunchtime. The other day, he told me that beneath the sparkling water is the path to Japan. He drools nonstop, and it's hard to understand his language. You have to be patient. There's too much medicine in him. They think the boy is crazy, but his head is just full of worms. He thinks too much. I found a pencil inside the house and gave it to him to draw. Mr. Olavo laid into me. What was I thinking, giving a sharp object to the boy, he said. It was dangerous for Ícaro, he could poke his eyes out. Poor boy. He gets stuck with things in his head. He doesn't know what to do with them. That's why he has this mad idea of crossing the ocean and going to Japan. Crazy boy.

I can't forget to take supplies from Dona Rosa's pantry. I'll steal the cans of food, but what I really want is to kill Dona Rosa.

LÁZARO SHOUTS:

Ícaro? You go to school every day and can't even talk. All you do is drool and fall. You're a retard, and I don't want to play with you because you're useless. When I grow up, I'll put you and all the crazy people in a loony bin.

You're a retard. Do you know how to speak English? What about German?

Du Dummkopf. Ich bin rein und klug.

ÍCARO THINKS:

The three neighbors never invited us over to their house to pick out herbs. They didn't offer *Cosme e Damião* goodie bags,[3] even though they were very religious. Besides none of the second-floor windows are ever opened. Whenever Lázaro had his singing and piano lessons, the ghosts' screams tried to make themselves heard. In my head, it was an almost unbearable noise. Grandma called an ambulance because I howled with fear at all the wailing and torment coming from the second floor. She explained to the doctors that I heard voices and that, with all the commotion from the singing and

---

3. Brazilian tradition, referring to the distribution of candies and sweets in paper bags to children around the time of Saints Cosmas and Damian festivities.

music coming from the neighbors, things got worse, and I started hearing screams. It was, Grandma explained, a reaction to the noise that I rejected, which made me imagine I was hearing screams and cries.

I know Grandma was telling the truth. Everything I heard was real—but only inside my head.

FATHER ARCANJO COMMENTS:

It's been over a month since the boys from the street were last seen. Íris keeps carrying on with her litany, claiming they were kidnapped, and everyone dismisses her. She keeps asking me what I know, but even if I did know something, I wouldn't say. A priest must always be discreet and not get involved in worldly matters.

Still, I keep a close eye on the children of Santa Graça. I go from house to house asking for information—if anyone has any clue, if the black boys have been seen anywhere.

One day, I even spoke to the police. The officers came to the parish's house. Outside, in the little square, Santa Graça's families strolled around, buying popcorn. Ícaro, poor thing, walked arm in arm with Dona Ondina so the other children wouldn't be afraid. When the boy took strong medication, saliva dripped from his mouth, something he couldn't control no matter how hard he tried. He struggled to keep that stuff in, twisting his tongue, but he wasn't able to. The whole town saw this sad, ugly sight, and the children were terrified of him. Dona Ondina held his arm to reassure the other mothers that everything was under control. Mr. Olavo never took his son out for walks—he was too busy. He sold books to the government: *Encyclopedia of Brazilian Eugenics*. He worked tirelessly, and some people didn't like it when he rang their doorbells, thinking he was a spy for the state. Those people need to pray more and think less. What harm can a white, honest man selling knowledge possibly do?

Despite my efforts, the police repeated that they didn't have the time or the manpower to go after runaway black boys. They'll come back at their own will since they managed to go so far, they told the mothers from

Mata Cavalo. Those who know how to leave also know how to return. I can't disagree.

FATHER ARCANJO THINKS
about Latin lessons for the town boys.

FATHER ARCANJO HAS
a fear of God.
a headache.

ÍCARO THINKS:

Mother and I returned from our walk in Matriz Square. The sky was closing in, a thick, heavy gray. As we arrived home, a flock of pigeons took off from the roof of the big house, squawking loudly. Mother said it was a bad omen.

I had a breakdown, yelled at Grandma, and they let me stay home instead of going to school. I hung from my bedroom window, watching Lázaro—that loathsome Lázaro. That morning, he was restless. He went to the back porch and brought a straw bag filled with bones—too big to belong to dogs.

He told me he had found a skeleton over the weekend and had spent Saturday and Sunday cleaning everything until the bones were pure white. Lázaro was building a skeleton from two tree trunks, and he planned to fill the mouth hole with a real tongue. Besides the bones, he also had eyes and even hearts in vinegar jars somewhere in the house. Dália warned me to be careful with all his lies. The boy made things up and probably got it from his real family, since no one really knew where he came from.

He also told me that later that day, after his German lesson, he would receive a reward from the old women in the house for doing so well in his Latin lessons with Father Arcanjo. The reward was also a birthday present, something really special. For the first time, he would skin an animal and debone it with his own hands to build a new skeleton—a big one, as human-like as possible. It will happen upstairs, he told me.

LÁZARO SHOUTS:

I'm going to build a skeleton with human bones. Ícaro, do you want to help me?

You can't play with me because I'm smart and you're retarded. *Du Dummkopf.*

Can't you take a joke, Ícaro? You have to take what I say with a grain of salt. But you're retarded and probably don't find anything funny. *Ich bin klug.*

ÍCARO THINKS:

I never stop watching from my window, waiting for the street boys to knock on the door at the big house. I kept the burnt-tasting black caramels that stick to your teeth. I keep an eye on the balcony. There are no more street games, no more tossing candy from the windows. I wait every day, but they don't come.

Out of the corner of my eye, I notice something surprising: a window on the upper floor is open. In all my thirteen years, I had never seen an open window on the second floor of that big house.

I run to get the caramels I saved for the black boy. I barely take two steps forward before I fall. I drag myself to my room and return with the wrappers clenched in my sweaty hands. I aim carefully at the open window on the second floor and throw them inside with precision. I hold my breath, waiting for something to happen— for someone to yell at me, for the pigeons living inside to burst out in fear, for the sharp sound of breaking glass to shatter the silence.

It doesn't take long. Something hits my shoulder, coming from the open window. Then another. And a third. I pick up the small bundles, wrapped in the same caramel paper.

Before I even open one, I already know it's not what I expected. Wrapped in each piece of delicate silk paper was a human tooth.

DR. LÍRIO AND MR. OLAVO TALK:

These people are gathering and getting organized. The Brazilian Black Front keeps multiplying, and now they have the Black Club for Social Culture, they have the Black Legion. Look at that, Olavo.

They're counting their chickens before they've hatched, and they won't get a single chicken out of it. You see, my friend, the Eugenics Movement is the only structured movement that can truly save the country from this kind of reaction. It's a worldwide and respected theory. Science is on our side, leaving no room for doubt. And if science wasn't enough to put them in their place, the Constitution guarantees us this fight.

As if science and the Constitution weren't already sufficient, our friends in São Paulo and the capital—intellectuals, doctors, journalists, well-educated and decent people—are publishing articles that need to be shared even more. The population must receive top-quality education. And we, who have access to these newspapers, books, and pamphlets, have an obligation to keep the people of Santa Graça and the region well-informed. And it's not just the *pardos*[4] and black people who hinder the proper development and progress of a country. Unfortunately for you, my friend, you must understand

OLAVO THINKS:
Fly, Ícaro, fly.

that defective children bring us no advantage in creating a purer, healthier, cleaner place. We all must pay a price for progress, my friend.

That black maid you have has been serving me increasingly lukewarm coffee, Olavo.

DR. LÍRIO HAS
a fear of God
a headache
a little bit of guilt.

---

4. *Pardos:* people of mixed racial identity

ÍRIS FEELS

sorry;

an urge to kill Dona Rosa, Dona Ondina, Dr. Lírio, Mr. Olavo, Lázaro, the witches—and to mix all the utensils together.

ÍCARO THINKS:

I clutched the bundles of teeth and thought about Lázaro and the gift he was going to receive, about the skeleton he was going to build. I ran as fast as I could, stumbling over my own legs through my mother's room, through the living room, and into my own bedroom, straight to the window—to find Lázaro. But what I really wanted was not to find Lázaro in the yard. Because if he wasn't there, then I would know for sure that he was the one who had thrown those teeth into the house. My frantic eyes, dreading the sight of him, scanned every corner. No sign of Lázaro. A chill ran through my spine, and my chest caved in when, after a few seconds, I spotted a tiny figure in the back of the yard, near the border with Mata Cavalo.

It was him. Lázaro was coming down the hill behind the big house, carrying a bag full of dead birds. He waved at me, called me a retard, and shouted that he had six dead sparrows in the bag, as well as another sack with bones so big they looked human. With all of that, he said, he was going to build a bird-man.

ÍRIS WHISPERS:
I was making your bed, Ícaro.
I found these teeth under your pillow.
What a naughty boy.
What is this, Ícaro?
Your grandmother is going to be furious.
Can you explain this to me?

ÍCARO STAYS
silent.

OLAVO MENTIONS TO ONDINA:
I won't take long. They need me in the region. There's no shortage of encyclopedias to sell.

Santa Graça will get the recognition it deserves from the capital and São Paulo. What we're doing here, Ondina, is quite advanced—truly innovative.

Unfortunately, there's no shortage of black folks wanting to become white. They do everything like us. They even support a government that wants to get rid of them. They're blind. They don't have the intelligence we do. Santa Graça will be the purest town in Brazil. What these people need is to pray and ask God for the kingdom of heaven if they want to rest.

Don't you think we're right, Ondina? I asked God for a sign. I believe we're doing good work. Don't you think so, too?

In this world, there's a pyramid, a hierarchy, an order that must be upheld. I don't write for newspapers, but without my work, no one would know where the enemy hides. One day, I'll receive a medal. We're on the right side of history, Ondina. You'll be proud of me. Now, come here. Come to me.

ONDINA SPREADS
her legs for Olavo,
but feels nothing.

OLAVO THINKS
of Íris.

ÍCARO THINKS:
I kept the teeth under my pillow. Three teeth wrapped in caramel wrapper. If I told Mother and Grandma, they would throw everything away, get angry, and threaten me with Helga—the lady who looks after the mad children. They would lock the door to Mother's balcony and forbid me from watching the neighbors. So I told Íris instead. She listened, afraid, but said the big house was haunted and that I should forget about the teeth, or else I'd end up

too scared to go to bed.

Íris takes care of me. She's not supposed to, she's here to cook and clean, but she strokes my hair, wipes my drool when I take my medicine, helps me walk without tripping over my own feet, and tells me stories. I haven't seen my father in almost a month. He travels the region, knocking on doors, offering the *Encyclopedia of Eugenics*. I'm proud of my father. And I feel sorry for him when people slam the door in his face.

LÁZARO SAYS:

Ícaro, get away from that window, you retard. Just wait until I grow up a little more and I'll become a politician. Then I'll send you straight to the loony bin. Tell Íris to hurry up and finish her work there, because there's a whole floor waiting for her to scrub over here. Maybe today she'll finally wash that black hand of hers properly and come out clean and pure?

Íris, black and dirty.
Ícaro, retarded.

ÍRIS THINKS:

Nobody here is rich, but they always find a way to afford my services. I must be really miserable to accept working while hearing insults in the house of these poor folks who think they're fancy. I get a few coins at the end of the month. I am given a time to arrive, but not a time to leave. I make up for the low pay by taking some bits, here and there, from the pantry. I enter through the small back gate and have a bathroom just for me, since, I guess, they think my shit stinks worse than theirs. I only eat after they finish lunch, using a separate fork and knife, because they must imagine my mouth carries disease. Dona Rosa and Dona Ondina don't say out loud that being black is a sickness, but I can't even touch them. And it isn't just the two of them who think like this. They say the newspapers that arrive here in Santa Graça publish the greatest thinkers, the ones promoting some sort of cleansing for the progress of the country.

    The black and the crazy are a disgrace to a village like Santa Graça, that wants to be a role model. My cousin Cornélio sends me letters from São Paulo and says things will get better for people of color, but that it's gonna take time. In the big city, there's a black newspaper. One with a name so beautiful it hurts: *Clarim da Alvorada*. But that paper is never gonna make it here. And even if it did, almost no black folks here know how to read. Only white newspapers have any use in this place.

> **DR. LÍRIO EXPLAINS:**
> Look, Dona Ondina, your son walking arm in arm with a black woman? The whole of Santa Graça would laugh at your family. We still don't know for sure, but there are certain risks

of contagion that haven't been fully confirmed yet. It's better to avoid it.

You should take Ícaro for a stroll yourself. Soon, Helga will be around to do it, but that black woman—I don't recommend it.

Tomorrow, I'll leave some flyers from our invaluable *Jornal da Eugenia* with Olavo. I know some little black ones haven't been seen for a while, but there are still a few around.

If they show up begging for food, make sure they slip the pamphlets under the doors of the houses in downtown Santa Graça. If there are any left, they can shove them under the doors in Mata Cavalo—but be careful not to waste paper, because those people don't read.

And if they do, they don't understand much.

DR. LÍRIO HAS

a fear of God;
a fear of black people;
doubts;
guilt.

FATHER ARCANJO COMMENTS:

The pamphlets explain that Santa Graça must follow the country's progressive trend, guided by the brightest minds—scientists and intellectuals—and fully embrace the eugenics cause.

Dr. Lírio takes great pride in being part of the eugenics committee that meets in São Paulo and Rio de Janeiro four times a year. He returns to Santa Graça full of ideas and enthusiasm. A man without doubts about his duty. This town is a pioneer in many initiatives that are paving the way for a much better country—free of contamination. It's unfortunate, but people like Íris would, little by little, disappear from the map. But that would take a while, because that black woman is still very useful. She is a highly trustworthy person who knows her place, fears God, and has access to the manor. She doesn't ask questions and stays silent. Discreet. Trustworthy.

FATHER ARCANJO HAS
a fear of God;
a heavy conscience;
his hand beneath his cassock;
desire for boys.

ÍCARO SAYS:
My mother told me I had to go to school. Grandma had a doctor's appointment in the big city and can't look after me. I asked to stay with Íris, but my mother wouldn't allow it. She warned me about the danger of being alone at home with a black woman. She could do all kinds of bad things, steal, hit me, and my mother didn't want to take any risks. So I had no choice but to go to school. I asked Íris to keep an eye on the neighbors and, if she saw any sign of the street boys, to tell me when I got back. At school, everything was as usual. I took my medicine to keep myself from banging my head against the wall, from shouting, from saying nonsense. As a result, I drooled all through the first part of the day. All my classmates pointed at me as I struggled to keep my tongue from slipping out of my mouth. Some of them are scared of me and cry. Those who cry get on my nerves because I don't want them to feel none of that for

me – I just want to be left alone. At recess, a teacher comes and sits next to me. There is a yellow-painted bench in front of the white ipe tree in the schoolyard, and that's where I sit. I dream about jumping from my bedroom window into the neighbor's duck tank. I know the water is deep, that a dive would make me float and take me away from the restlessness caused by the other children. But none of that would ever be possible because, besides taking too much medication, I am never left alone. Only Íris listens to me. Only she knows about this dream.

I sat on the yellow bench for the whole recess, rocking my head and legs. My thick drool fell down my chin, and my curled tongue kept me from speaking properly. I was a pitiful, terrifying sight. I put my trembling hands over my face to hide it, but my crooked fingers only made me look even more like a monster. I had tried so many times to stop taking my medicine because my mouth scared the others, and I was ashamed of that. But my mother and grandmother always caught me when I tried to hide the pills.

The recess ended, and I got in line – last as always. I got nervous when the teacher said we were going to do group work. Every time that happens, I get upset and start looking for a wall to bang my head against. The kids always go out of their way to make sure I don't end up in their groups. The teacher picks five children, and they take turns choosing classmates until the groups are formed. While this is happening, I clasp my hands together and try to cover my mouth, hiding the drool that keeps falling. Damn medicine! I cover my mouth and stomp my twisted feet, turned inward, one over the other. I must really scare the other kids because no one ever picks me. By the time it's over, I'm the only one left. By then, I'm already soaked in piss, reeking, because I get too nervous. They take me to the office and leave me there until someone comes to pick me up and take me home. That day, with my mother at work and my father traveling to sell encyclopedias, only Íris was left. When she arrived to pick me up, she hugged me. Íris's hug is the best thing that has ever happened to me. That afternoon, I tried to die, but Íris wouldn't let me.

LÁZARO SHOUTS:
Icaro, you pissed yourself at school again? You retard! *Du bist einfach dumm.*

ÍRIS THINKS:
There goes that boy to bed, all tied up and full of medicine. Under his pillow, three teeth wrapped in the silk paper left from the burnt-tasting black caramel. Soon, Dr. Lírio will come to check on him. The doctor speaks near the boy, saying how unlucky it is that he is slow in the head because, with such fair skin, he could procreate when he grew up, making the country a more dignified, purer place. I've gotten used to hearing these things. I live with the urge to kill these people, and I don't even know exactly why. I just need to pray more, to go confess to the holy Father. Dr. Lírio barely arrived to see the boy before suggesting that Dona Ondina consider that Helga take care of him. He said she would soon be looking for another household to work for. A woman of great trust, highly qualified to look after defective boys and girls. She knew all the medicines, had studied chemistry, and was highly regarded by the priest. A white woman, rosy-skinned, blue-eyed, blonde-haired. It would be an enormous stroke of luck for Ícaro to have Helga around. They absolutely didn't want me staying with the boy. The medical recommendation was for as little contact as possible, as explicitly stated in some papers from São Paulo. One accepts it because that's just how life is, but that doesn't mean I don't feel like killing these people.

ÍCARO HEARS:

Lázaro playing the piano and singing. At that very moment, voices, screams, and cries echo from the second floor.

ÍCARO THINKS:

Grandma insisted that my delirium was caused by my strong medication, but if I took everything correctly, I would stop hearing so much nonsense and would only hear Lázaro's voice and piano.

While I slept under so much medication, Grandpa's ghost appeared. He left me clues, and that night he told me to keep the teeth wrapped in caramel silk paper and to listen to Jão da Lavagem. There was something in common there. He also spoke about Father Arcanjo and his Sunday lunches. I woke up and vomited a lot. I needed to get up. I wanted to understand what Grandpa's message meant. I managed to get out of bed while Mom was at work and Grandma was baking a cake. Íris untied me and told me that if there was any trouble, I should say I managed to free myself. Íris really needs this job. At five in the afternoon, Jão da Lavagem came slowly with his donkey pulling the cart, shouting to the residents of Santa Graça: "Who's got *lavagem*?" Outside the big house, Lobélia and Alpínia waited for the man with two cans of fat. He thanked them many times. He left, and the old women returned to the wood stove. From my room, I saw what was happening in the kitchen. In the pot, a stew. Inside the pot, a heel. They must have been preparing the pig for lunch with Father Arcanjo.

ÍCARO SEES
Lázaro reading the *Eugenics Bulletin*.

ÍCARO THINKS:
Lázaro reads a lot. *The Eugenics Bulletin*. He is very intelligent, Lázaro.

He saw me. He asked if I had finally learned how to walk and then burst into his usual laughter after asking me anything. Lázaro laughs a lot. He put down the newspaper and told me that the three old women were cooking an entire lamb for Sunday. He also said he was assembling a skeleton as close to a human as possible. He was missing the teeth and the skull. Those were hard to get because Father Arcanjo wouldn't allow it. A human head was sacred. He said God would punish anyone who played with such things.

DONA ROSA SPEAKS LOUDLY:

Santa Graça is on the radio. Listen, Ondina. They're talking about the runaway little blacks. A lawyer from the region wants to investigate, they say. Apparently, the lawyer wants to go door to door in downtown Santa Graça to see if he can find traces of the boys. A waste of time—by now, they must be living the good life in another town. Surely, they got involved with drugs. They were raised too freely. Their mothers, instead of taking care of them, work in the houses downtown. And you see what happens. The children grow up without a foundation, right? And this is the result. Let this be a lesson, right, Ondina? God protect us from such misfortunes!

ÍRIS THINKS:

Dona Rosa and Dona Ondina deserve to die. I need to pray more.

ÍRIS SPITS

into the rice pudding she serves to Dona Rosa and Dona Ondina. They love it.

ÍRIS THINKS:

My mother worked in downtown Santa Graça. As expected, I also went to work in the town center. Our home has always been in Mata Cavalo. We take care of other people's children, cook fresh and delicious meals for families, clean houses, and tend to gardens we will never have.

My love has always been João Marcolino. Jão, like myself, worked as a servant since he was a boy, collecting *lavagem* from the houses of Santa Graça. He became an orphan at seven and always lived in a shack on our street, surrounded by the pigs that became his livelihood. He was always the best swine supplier in town, even better than those from the mayor's farm. When the mayor noticed Jão's dedication to his work, he suggested that he work for him. In exchange, he would receive medical care and a slightly better shack. Instead, what really happened was that Jão had to give the mayor half the price of his pigs and still had to stand in line at the hospital like every other poor person, whether it was to treat *bicho de pé*,[5] or a nasty cough. Jão never questioned life. He never went to school and lived there, content, because that's just how it was supposed to be.

I caught his gaze on a hot afternoon, during a street dance. Jão, already grown, was puffing on a straw cigarette outside his shack. When he saw me staring at him stubbornly, he took two swigs of *cachaça*[6] and came to talk to me. We started dating. When Jão proposed, I was already expecting

---

5. Portuguese colloquial term for the jigger flea: parasitic insect that burrows into the skin causing pain and potentially infection.
6. Distilled spirit made from fermented sugarcane juice.

our baby. I dreamed of our little black boy with green eyes, just like Jão's. But the child never came. He even had a name: Joaquim. Joaquim turned into a terrible appendicitis. When I went to Dr. Lírio and he saw the pregnancy, he ordered an operation. He said it looked like a fetus, but it was an infected appendix, and my great luck was that he performed the surgery right there. When the appendix came out, Joaquim came with it.

Dr. Lírio was also a good man at that moment: he wrapped the baby in straw and handed him to me. He ordered me to bury him. And there he is, beneath the banana tree. Jão and I kept trying, but no child ever came after Joaquim.

I couldn't get it out of my head. After my surgery, the black women from Mata Cavalo started coming down with appendicitis too. Dr. Lírio and Father Arcanjo went to our neighborhood, inviting each one to the hospital, offering free hot meals in their rooms while they recovered. They even said there was an appendicitis epidemic. But people like us, who never studied, didn't know that it was all lies. When a young man from the city's health clinic came to visit us, he said the whole story about an appendicitis epidemic was strange because it wasn't something that spread from one person to another. Contagious or not, and at the holy Father's request, I convinced the black women of Mata Cavalo that anyone under thirty needed to go to the hospital and get their appendix checked. Everyone was hungry and desperate for a proper bed to sleep in, so they all went in for surgery.

In exchange, I was promised money to buy a house in downtown Santa Graça. The amount was, however, never enough. I dreamed of so many things. When I was very little, my mother would warn us black girls to be careful because the traveling circus that passed through town kidnapped girls like me. They made them disappear. I always dreamed of running away with the circus. On the radio, I heard about the *Companhia Negra de Revista*—a group of people like me who left to join the circus and lived for singing. But no circus ever comes through Santa Graça. My mother was wrong. Nothing ever happens here. So now, my dream is a proper house in the center of town. I deserve it, after all.

ÍCARO THINKS:
Sleep won't come.

It's already past ten. The house is silent. Only my grandfather's ghost is in my room.

I get up from bed and open the window. Down below, there's the water tank where the ducks and geese from the big house drink from. The water that should be deep, that would take me to the other side of the earth. I spread my arms to fly. But I stop, startled, when I see a figure in a long black robe carrying a bag. I grab my flashlight from the hole in the broken wood of the windowsill and shine it in the intruder's face. Under the hood—Father Arcanjo. He lowers his head and runs toward the side gate, carrying the heavy-

looking bag. I am afraid. I want to die, but
I don't want to be killed—especially not
by Father Arcanjo.

ÍRIS, ÍCARO, LÁZARO, THE THREE SISTERS, OLAVO, DR. LÍRIO, DONA ROSA, DONA ONDINA, FATHER ARCANJO, AND THE ENTIRE TOWN HEAR:

Good afternoon, dear listeners. The Department of Press and Propaganda will now broadcast the National Program on this September 7th from the Vasco da Gama Rowing Club Stadium in the Rio de Janeiro neighborhood of São Januário, where, every year, the Brazilian people gather to hear the speeches of President Getúlio Vargas.

The Brazilian people, in their full exercise of decency, must promote and support sanitation, eugenics, and hygiene policies for the broad dissemination of modern measures proclaimed by the *Pro-Sanitation League* and the *Mental Hygiene League* for the full development of Brazilian society. The President of Brazil and all upstanding Brazilian families must understand the importance of eugenic policy as a means of improving the Brazilian people. It is urgent to spread this scientific advancement, already in full development and use in First World countries.

According to the Constitution of the United States of Brazil, dated 1934:

Article 138 — It is the duty of the Union, the states, and the municipalities to:
- Promote eugenic education;
- Ensure mental hygiene and encourage the fight against social poisons.

OLAVO SAYS:
Santa Graça will one day be a reference on the Brazilian map. Our eugenics policy is one of the boldest and most advanced.

The day of our recognition will come. The most important thing is the seed we are planting.

Where's the maid? Have you seen how dirty the garage is, Ondina?

OLAVO THINKS;
about Íris;
about Íris's dark body;
poor Íris.

ÍCARO THINKS:
After seeing Father Arcanjo wandering the big house at dawn, I started waking up drenched in sweat, terrified he would come into my house.

Two days later, early on a Sunday, before Mass, someone knocked on the door.

It was him.

Íris didn't work on Sundays—she wouldn't be able to help me.

From my room, I heard the priest say he would have lunch there with the old women and that I should be ready at five in the afternoon. We would go together to the parish house for a much needed exorcism. He told my parents that I had been spying from out the window and disrupting the order of Santa Graça, and that made God very angry with me.

(**Noon**)

By that time, Father Arcanjo had already finished Mass and was probably arriving at the old women's house.

(**2:48 PM**)

The clock showed nearly three in the afternoon. Father Arcanjo clapped his hands outside, and my mother told him to come in. I was sitting on my bed, freshly bathed, my hair neatly parted to the side, waiting for the priest to take me away—to rid me of the demon.

I was terrified that my father would hit me because if something was wrong, he would get angry. The ghost of my grandpa once told me that I should be careful around my father and be happy when he left to sell encyclopedias. In a dream, Grandpa told me that when I was a baby, my father had flown into a rage because someone had snitched on him about a black family that had completely vanished from Santa Graça. He had gone to their house to sell books, and by coincidence—or not—they disappeared from the town just hours later. When he got home, he beat my mother and shook me so hard that I lost my breath. Grandpa caught him in the act and rushed me to the hospital. Since then, I've had to take medicine, and my feet stumble, and I don't walk too well. The medication also fills my head with thoughts that no one understands. When I told these things to Íris, I think I scared her, but she would just laugh and tell me it was all a dream. She said I should stop eating popcorn with melted cheese in the square at night—cheese makes you dream.

My heart jumped into my throat when I heard my father climbing the stairs. He was definitely coming to talk to me—to hit me, to yell. He came with my mother, and behind her was Father Arcanjo.

I hid under the sheet. I clutched the three teeth that kept me company and shut my eyes. My father opened the door and ordered me to sit up. I was so scared that I pretended to be dead. He then grabbed me by the arm, yanked me into a sitting position, and shouted at me to act like a man. Father Arcanjo watched me and made the sign of the cross. He said he was certain the devil had taken up residence inside me and that an exorcism was urgent.

He would expect me that Sunday at five in the afternoon, after Lázaro's lessons were done. He hoped that after the ritual, I wouldn't have to be institutionalized and would start behaving properly. My father squeezed my arm so hard that I started crying out in pain. I let out a scream and dropped the three human teeth that had been keeping me company. They scattered across the floor, rattling like loose stones from a broken necklace.

Horrified, Father Arcanjo pulled a crucifix from his pocket and shouted for Satan to leave me. The human teeth, he was certain, were proof that I knew things I shouldn't, and that was more than enough reason for me to be placed under Helga's care. She would soon be available and would gladly take care of me. Time to put an end to this nonsense, the Father declared.

FATHER ARCANJO EXPLAINS:

Mr. Olavo and Mrs. Ondina, the boy Ícaro is out of control. We will take care of him, but Helga must come. She will come gladly, as soon as she finishes her current work. Tomorrow, I will send a message to the mayor, asking him to send us this most capable young woman to look after the boy Ícaro.

I will take these teeth with me. May God have mercy on this child.

I expect you at five.

OLAVO THINKS:
Fly, Ícaro, fly.
Die, boy, die.

OLAVO SHOUTS:
Walk properly, boy, we're late. Stop stumbling. Walk properly, Ícaro. Stop drooling.

ÍCARO THINKS:

A little before five, I left the house for the exorcism. My mother held me by the arm and my father walked quickly ahead of us. I was angry, nervous, and my legs were betraying me. I was drooling a lot, too. My father was ashamed and angry. He slapped me as I walked, telling me to walk like a normal person. The more he said this, the more I stumbled, and he thought I was doing it to provoke him.

My father knocked on the door at the parish house, the priest opened up and told us to wait in the room. There were only two chairs in a simple room, just as God wanted. Through the crack in the door, I saw Lázaro. He was naked, lying on the bed, face down. From inside, the priest's fiery eyes met mine. He came into the room and said that Lázaro was resting. The boy wasn't feeling well, maybe from working his brain too hard. The priest, being a man of God, needed to let the child rest when he noticed intensive brain work. He made the sign of the cross as he touched my hand and told my parents to take me to the sacristy.

I had never been to the sacristy. For a while, I wanted to be an altar boy, but the priest wouldn't accept me. He said I was a fool and that with legs as crooked as mine, I would eventually drop some sacred object.

I sat on an old chair, facing the image of the dead Christ. There was so much I wanted to tell Íris, and that Sunday felt like the longest day of my life. I was going to ask her to hide me in her house, because if not, Helga would come to take care of me. I was sure that one day the little black boys from the street would return to play with the caramels, those with burnt taste that stick to the teeth.

After wetting his hands with holy water, Father Arcanjo asked my parents to leave us alone, as the exorcism would only work that way. I started vigorously stomping my foot, my tongue tied out of fear of the priest. My parents left quickly, and he asked me to take off my clothes, as a sign of humility before God. I shook my head, no. I clung to the cloth on the table, struggling to keep him from touching me. In addition to fear, I was disgusted by Father Arcanjo, who always ate pork stew and had white drool at the corners of his mouth. He grabbed my fingers hard, trying to pry them off the tablecloth. At that moment, he got really close to me, pressing his chest to my head and his leg to my thigh. Out of nervousness, I crawled under the table, and that's when I saw the bag the priest always carried, filled to the brim with large and small, thin and wide pieces of whitish sticks.

A WEEK BEFORE ÍCARO'S EXORCISM, ÍCARO, ÍRIS, THE THREE SISTERS, OLAVO, DR. LÍRIO, DONA ONDINA, DONA ROSA, FATHER ARCANJO, AND HELGA ALL HEAR:
Radio Minas reports:

The police in the town of Monte Novo, in the state of Minas Gerais, seized a clandestine human bone bank. Two *pardos* were arrested on the spot. The two individuals stated that they worked at the cemetery, cleaning the remains that were sold to doctors and dentists. When questioned by the police, the local doctor and dentist denied any involvement. The two *pardos* were jailed in the municipal prison.

ÍCARO THINKS:
I screamed so much and hit my head so hard under the table that my mother appeared in the sacristy. I was shirtless because Father Arcanjo had torn it off, and blood was dripping from my head. The priest shouted for my mother to leave the room, claiming that at that very moment, he was fighting against the devil inside me. He told her that I had even wanted to take my clothes off, proof that Satan and shamelessness were attacking me. I wanted to scream that it was a lie, but my tongue was tied, and I couldn't say anything. My father arrived, and Father

Arcanjo suggested that Dr. Lírio should pay me a visit. Besides the black people, the sick ones were also in Santa Graça, disrupting the purification project. He told my parents to reconsider the use of my existence. A sick child like me, in addition to scaring the normal children, was too much trouble with hallucinations and false accusations. Besides being unreliable, I was a financial burden on my parents.

I don't remember falling asleep. When I woke up, I was weak. I tried to get up but fell down—my legs wouldn't obey me. It was Monday, and I heard Íris's voice as she washed the porch. When she came to clean my room, I told her everything that had happened and begged her to take me away. She smiled—maybe out of pity. I knew it was far too risky for her to take me away from home.

ÍCARO HEARS:
Helga will come to take care of him.

ÍRIS THINKS:
This pale boy needs some sun. I'll put him by the window to watch the ducks, keep an eye on that sneaky Lázaro, and admire the water tank—he keeps saying that thing will take him all the way to Japan.

We, who aren't the mothers of those little black kids, have already gotten used to their disappearances. Where did those boys go without a trace?

ÍCARO THINKS:

Where did the boys go without leaving a trace?

I made a sign to Íris to put me by the window so I could see the big house, the three old women, Lázaro, the ducks, the shimmering water tank that flows to the other side of the ocean.

I sat on a chair high enough to see and stayed there, watching the sun hit the muddy water. Have the boys' mothers already gotten used to it? Why doesn't Íris have children?

ÍRIS PLACES

her hand on her belly;
her pitying eyes on Ícaro.

ÍRIS WHISPERS TO ÍCARO:

I once carried a child in my belly, but Dr. Lírio operated on me. The doctor said I had appendicitis, but I didn't feel any pain anywhere. Even so, he insisted on operating. After a long time, I tried and tried to have a child with Jão, but I never could. I wasn't the first nor the last to be operated on for appendicitis by Dr. Lírio. Everyone who went through surgery couldn't, in the end, carry a child. It was as if God was punishing all of us poor folks from Mata Cavalo. My Joaquim, who came out still in a little bundle, is buried beneath the banana tree near my house. Poor thing, he came out along with my appendix.

ÍCARO THINKS:

The voices from the big house continued, and I spent the week feeling very nervous, unable to get up from bed or the chair on my own. The howls from the second floor were so loud in my head that I cried, covering my mouth as if trying to silence all the screams I heard. Íris heard them too, but my mother, father, and grandmother didn't hear anything. They said the black woman couldn't be trusted and that my mind was completely failing. If we followed the recommendations of Father Arcanjo and Dr. Lírio, I would be much better off under Helga's care. But Grandpa didn't like her. I dreamed of him telling me that she didn't like children.

That Monday, after lunch, I asked Íris to take me back to the window. From there, I could see the wood stove. Lázaro told me his three mothers made an excellent *feijoada*,[7] and there was never a shortage of ears, feet, and noses. Snouts, he quickly

---

7. *Feijoada* is a traditional Brazilian stew made primarily with black beans and a variety of pork and beef cuts.

corrected, laughing.

What was cooking nonstop on the three old women's wood stove? Why was the fire never put out? Why was the fat that Jão da Lavagem carried from there thicker than fresh paint? Grandpa wasn't appearing anymore to tell me.

OLAVO TALKS WITH HELGA
(no one hears).

OLAVO SEES
Íris on all fours, scrubbing the bathroom.

OLAVO THINKS:
Fly, Ícaro, fly. Die already, boy!

ÍCARO HEARS
Íris saying we had a visitor. She told me Helga had arrived to see me, that I shouldn't be afraid, and that she would always keep an eye on the *polaca*.[8]

ÍRIS THINKS:
Dona Rosa ordered me to clean the guest room for the blondie who was moving into the house. Change the sheets—use the best ones—freshen the air, open the windows, and let the sun in. She told me to bake a cake, make juice—it was

---

8. *Polaca* is a colloquial term referring to light skinned, blond women.

like the emperor of the world was coming to visit. Clean the bathroom so the blonde could take her shit, an important, noble shit, not like mine. I had such a strong urge to kill that old woman. God forgive me.

DONA ROSA HAS:
disgust toward Íris;
anger toward Íris;
old clothes and stale food to give to Íris.

DONA ONDINA THINKS:
Helga—short in stature, long trousers, always wearing a buttoned-up long-sleeved shirt, and hands clasped at her stomach. She said she had arrived in Santa Graça a long time ago. Some said she was German, others whispered that she had fled a convent school, and others insisted she came from the capital, where she had trained to be a nurse. Her blonde hair was tied up in a greasy bun that never moved. She also had a thick and generous mustache, blonde too, but darker than the hair on her head, contrasting with her rosy skin.

DONA ONDINA SAYS:
Welcome, my dear. What a beautiful young lady! Such eyes! Make yourself at home. Ícaro is eager to meet you.

DONA ROSA THINKS
about how white Helga's hands are; about the disgust she feels for Íris.

LÁZARO SHOUTS:
Has Helga arrived yet, retard? At least now you won't have to put your hands on that black Íris. Helga is white like me. She's clean. Maybe now you'll learn to walk properly. Have you seen the skeleton I built? I got teeth and other bones that Father Arcanjo saved for me.

ÍCARO AND ÍRIS WATCH
Alpínia coming down to the bottom of the hill, weaving between the banana trees. She was covered in blood and carrying a large sack on her back. When she saw them, she ordered them away from the window. She yelled at them not to spy on other people's lives, saying they were overstepping their limits. She tried to explain that the sack held ducks and drakes for the Sunday roast. Someone had to slaughter the animals if they wanted to eat them. No one did it better than her. It wasn't long before Alpínia returned to the edge of Mata Cavalo. This time, she had half a dozen more sacks, full of meat and blood. It was for the banquet. The skin, boiled for hours on the wood-burning stove, turned into fat. While watching the old woman, the screams from the second floor of the big house only grew louder—just barely drowned out by Lázaro's piano and singing lesson.

ÍCARO THINKS:
Íris helps me lean forward to see the rainbow in the water of the duck pond. She holds onto my legs, but I don't feel anything. She holds me so I don't fall. If I fell into that, I'd surely end up in Japan, crossing the ocean. But the sun in my eyes makes everything too bright, without clarity. I lean forward more. I'm sure Íris is holding me down, not back.

When Helga arrived, Íris and I didn't move. She kept holding me near the window. The blonde woman approached, said her name, and I tried to introduce myself, but my tongue wouldn't even let me say my own name. Helga was scandalized by the intimacy between me and Íris. A black woman clinging to a white child's legs—how could they allow such a thing? Helga shouted for Íris to let go of me, saying that from now on, she would take care of me. Íris resisted, gripping my legs tightly. Helga kept trying to pull her away. In the struggle between the two, I felt my fingertips grow wet, and a breathlessness overtook me, as if I were truly alive. The shimmer of sunlight on the muddy water grew brighter as my arms pierced the surface. Íris told me to be at peace because

I was finally reaching the other side of the world. Maybe that was where the street kids had gone. That was when I felt my legs slip free, and I plunged entirely into the glistening water.

As I stretched my fingers—now longer and longer—toward the colors and the light in the water, I began to float downwards, sinking into the earth like I was flying toward Japan. At some point, I must have bumped into something because I stopped floating. I was standing. I was no longer crawling, and my voice was smooth. I opened my eyes, and before me stood the lost children of Santa Graça. One had been thrown down the stairs, another suffocated with a pillow, one with her head split open from a fall in the bathroom, and a girl carrying tiny rubber fish clutched in her hands. A breath on my back. A burst of laughter. When I turned around, I saw the boy with the caramels. So this was where he had been hiding—on his way to Japan! I smiled. He smiled back. Inside his mouth, all his teeth were missing.

Delfina Bittencourt

DELFINA DREAMS
of becoming a doctor.

DELFINA THINKS:
My family was torn apart by money. We had plenty, and we had pedigree. Just look at me. With these eye and hair colors, I know the surnames of my great-great-grandparents all the way back to the 16th century. Unlike black people, who are only children of their parents, if that. They are never grandchildren or great-grandchildren of anyone.

I was thirteen when my parents died. Both were shot inside our own home. The ones who killed them were a black couple who took care of the garden and the house. They had everything an employee could dream of. They lived rent-free in a well-kept little house with a view of the reservoir. They didn't pay rent; in exchange, they worked to afford that good life. My mother even turned a blind eye when a few coins went missing from the kitchen jar, when the pantry emptied faster than expected. It was fine, we were born to be good and to love our neighbor, as we learned without fail every Sunday.

Still, they killed my parents. Surely, they never read the word of God. *Thou shalt not kill.* There is no greater ingratitude. We gave them everything, and at the first opportunity—betrayal, murder and the destruction of a good family.

I was a boarding student at Colégio Santa Catarina, the most prestigious school in the region. A convent school, with an education that came at a high price. When they heard about my parents' murder, the nuns offered me a full scholarship since I was an excellent student. I became a charity case. Until I graduated, I would have full support, and they treated me as a new member of the family.

The nuns took such good care of me that I never spent a night without sleeping with them. I took turns. Some nights, I stayed with Sister Raquel, others with Sister Débora, some days with Sister Adélia, or Sister Sara. They all caressed me until I calmed down. I missed my parents. Sister Raquel was my favorite. She stroked my hair, my legs, my breasts. Sometimes, Sister Adélia would arrive unexpectedly and share the affection with Sister Raquel. They locked the door with the latch and caressed the fine, blonde hairs growing between my thighs. They giggled and whispered in my ear, wet licks that made me explode inside. Sister Raquel liked to help with my long baths, almost an hour long. When I was tired, they promised I didn't have to do anything. They just wanted to play with me. I would stretch out on the bed, they played at changing my clothes as if I were a doll, and I would fall asleep with my thighs wet, pulsing. Whenever Mother Superior visited the school, I had to sleep alone. That was bad because then I had no company. Each of us went to our own room, and there was an absolute silence in the hallway, which was usually filled with giggles and doors softly closing throughout the night.

DELFINA READS:
Next station — Santa Graça.

DELFINA THINKS:
I spent many years at the boarding school. There was only one year left before I finished my studies, and the plan was for me to move to the capital. My dream was to be a nurse, but my uncle had already arranged for me to marry a distant cousin.

Chemistry was my passion. If I could, I would have become a doctor, but being a nurse would have been enough. It seemed, however, that I was destined to be a housewife. At school, I studied the periodic table, knew a lot about all sorts of experiments, and was considered the best student in the subject.

Cursed be the rainy day when a black woman ruined the plans my uncle had for me. The school was closed for visitors, and only the boarders were in their rooms. It wasn't yet dinnertime, but it was an acceptable hour to bathe. Sister Raquel was giving me a long bath, soaping my legs and thighs, when one of the housemaids, a black woman named Cássia, God damn her, burst into the bathroom, breathless and running frantically, with my uncle right behind her. The moment she saw me naked beside Sister Raquel, who was also unclothed, her head shaved, without her habit, her breasts exposed, time stopped.

I packed my bags under my uncle's stern gaze. On the way to the station, before his train departed, he abandoned me, forbidding me from following him. I considered going back to the school, but I was certain I wouldn't be welcomed. Sister Raquel wouldn't last much longer before being sent off to some faraway town to serve another purpose. What expression did our faces hold when they saw us together? I sat alone on the bench at the station. When I looked around and saw no one on the platform, I realized I was free. I had no money, nowhere to go, and no family. I had no age, no qualifications, no past, and no future. My head felt like it was about to explode, so I made up a story. I told myself the tale I would repeat for the rest of my life. I gave myself a new name and became a nurse.

On the train, the last stop is Santa Graça.

On the train, heels together. I press my legs tightly shut. I know I will never feel anything between them again. I will miss Sister Raquel. My name is Helga Tatler. I am a nurse, descended from a family of German immigrants who were murdered by black people. I have extensive experience caring for children, and I've never been without work. I was raised with strict discipline and patriotism by Catholic nuns. A role model. Having me around is, unquestionably, a privilege. Sister Raquel was no older than twenty-five. Her hands roamed my body daily, sliding with a locked-up desire that, out of sheer bad luck, had forgotten to lock itself away that afternoon, in a moment of haste. Our intimacy was exposed before my uncle and the black woman. We covered ourselves with sheets and towels, only to hear my uncle say that his daughter was dead and that I should get ready for the funeral in the capital. The train would leave in two hours—there was no time to waste.

I replay this story in my memory over and over again, countless times. On the seat beside me, a copy of a publication from São Paulo. A curious and highly interesting article about the purification of the Brazilian nation. Intellectuals of great prestige, good, enlightened people debated the concept of eugenics. A rich bulletin filled with ideas of great progress and nobility. The natural selection of races should be promoted, in accordance with the Constitution of the United States of Brazil, distributed among households across the country so that everyone would understand the consequences of so much racial mixing: physical and mental diseases, unhappiness, rejection by society. It was possible to live in a happy country, where everyone felt they belonged to a superior community, free from the mentally and physically ill. As I read these revolutionary ideas, I felt an immense pride in my appearance. Indeed, those ideas from São Paulo were not to be questioned, since their meaning and purpose were very clear. They were to be obeyed, all for the well-being of the nation. I placed the *Bulletin of Eugenics* in my suitcase. Once again, I forgot my past, my name, and rehearsed my story once more, this time with a small correction: my extensive experience in caring for children was specifically focused on defective children.

I got off at Santa Graça Station. A role model of a town, filled with families of German surnames, something of true importance. The ticket collector, a *pardo*, explained to me that skin like his would soon disappear. He had married a white woman, following the advice of Father Arcanjo, a very holy man, and his children already had much lighter skin and would have many more opportunities. His black mother? He hadn't seen her in years, she had vanished with not so much as a word. His sisters? They had disappeared along with the mother. Nothing to worry about, though. It was common for them to move away, to try their luck elsewhere. Santa Graça had once had many *pardos* and black people, but now it was becoming harder and harder to spot a street kid, thank God, he said.

Things were improving—no more little black children begging for stale bread, and the older ones either died young or left town. The feeble-minded also didn't last long—poor creatures. There were still defective children in town, but they didn't survive long. Weak health, you know. The eugenicist ideas had already reached Santa Graça, and I could work there as a nurse. I asked for the address of the church.

Sitting on one of the benches of the main church, Bible in hand, was Father Arcanjo. The loud echo of my heels on the empty altar made the holy man turn. He adjusted his glasses. Then he immediately asked for my surname. Tatler. I am a nurse for mad children, with vast experience. My parents are dead. Without family and without the means to pay for a life on my own, I took a ride to Santa Graça and hope to be useful in this parish. It wasn't convenient for a young, strong girl like me to be without purpose. I am also looking for a house that can shelter me, and in return, I can dedicate my time to caring for the defective. If everyone in Santa Graça is perfect, then tell me, so I can be useful in another parish. I came to you because I have faith in Jesus. God is above all, amen.

Father Arcanjo told me that I was very welcome and that I should stay under his and God's care until he spoke to some families who would embrace with enthusiasm someone who would take the burden of caring for a defective child, and, therefore, would not be able to reproduce good and healthy children. He said I should go with him to the parish house to settle in.

The Father left, and at the parish house, two *pardas* stayed with me— I'm not sure if they had names—whose ages seemed to be similar to mine. They were good at their work. They prepared the bathtub with hot water, soap, a clean towel, a table with cake, jams, bread, and *pitanga* juice. They made fresh coffee when I asked, with whole milk, and biscuits. I cleaned myself, ate, and got dressed. I should be ready for any opportunity that might surface from that moment on. I wore a solid blue dress, my hair still damp, tightly pinned into a stiff bun. Even I thought I looked like a Helga.

Since the Father didn't return, I took the chance to appreciate the simple room that would be mine for the coming days. A Bible on the bedside table, a table covered with a crochet cloth and made of dark wood. A large rosary hanging on the wall above the single bed. A small bookshelf with a few books: *Essay on the Inequality of the Human Races* by Gobineau, *Hereditary Genius* by Francis Galton, and *The Passing of the Great Race* by Madison Grant caught my attention, and I realized that Father Arcanjo read in other languages. In my suitcase, some books I had would enrich that small collection. In boarding school, we never had the means to buy books, but we visited the library often. Some titles were true passions that I read again and again, wishing for them to be mine, which is why I stole them, or they were stolen for me as gifts late at night while some of the nuns and I played doctor. Those volumes were part of my dream to become a nurse. *The Bible of Health* and *Eugenics, and*

Social Medicine were my favorites. Others I read compulsively just for fun: *Frankenstein*, *The Strange Case of Dr. Jekyll and Mr. Hyde*, and *The Island of Dr. Moreau*.

When Father Arcanjo returned from the street, he was delighted with my refined taste in literature. I, Helga Tatler, had learned to appreciate all that erudition in the Sanitary Education course at the Institute of Health and Hygiene on Brigadeiro Tobias Street, in São Paulo.

DELFINA RESENTS
a lot.

DELFINA MISSES
Sister Raquel.

LÁZARO STUDIES
hard;
to become mayor.

FATHER ARCANJO COMMENTS:
One could say that she is a true Fraulein! Fraulein Tatler, Helga, is the lady's name. A young lady of the best

nature, who came from an excellent family and background and, through God's will became an orphan. Luck, however, does not leave us and Santa Graca was blessed with the arrival of such a suitable young woman into town and who was at the disposal of the ones who needed her. A nurse specialized in handicapped children.

FATHER ARCANJO THINKS
of little boys.

DELFINA THINKS:
Father Arcanjo, that holy man with a heart of gold, let me rest the entire day. He took me to see the garden of the parish house and told me about the plants that grew there. He showed me the pitanga tree, the mango tree, and the pear trees. He was very proud of the strawberries, fruits from temperate climates that, unlike mangoes, made us more civilized. It was enough to look at how a mango is eaten and how a strawberry is savored. The difference was enormous. One is a rough fruit, the other a refinement. Even in this, the more temperate regions of the

Earth have the advantage, but we here in Santa Graça are working tirelessly. We will rid ourselves of all the impurity of the world, the filth of miscegenation, the burden and horror that are physical and mental defects, and that I, Helga, was an angel for falling in the right place.

The Father returned from his outing with good news. The whole town already knew of my arrival. A young woman of such pure race couldn't arrive in Santa Graça without drawing attention, and the mayor was expecting us for a reception at the end of the afternoon. All the respectable families were invited, and some had already shown interest in my work. Despite significant progress, Santa Graça still had some defective children, and I could take care of them without any problem.

When leaving the parish house, I noticed several little black boys playing in the street. Father Arcanjo, in a low voice, signaled that those children would soon disappear from the town. Not out of malice, but because in Santa Graça, there was no function for which they could serve.

FATHER ARCANJO EXPLAINS:

Many leave, fleeing of their own will, and unfortunately, the parents of these boys have the habit of blaming the authorities for the disappearance of their little black ones, poor devils. If they attended mass, they might even be heard, but they are different people, they have connections with spirits through drumming dances, things that Jesus condemns. They cultivate herbs, make potions. They are, in fact, very different from us. It's not easy to convince them of this, but the Constitution already warns us, and we support the president, his government, because we want the country to succeed. And who can stand against science? All this theory is proven in books about eugenics. If only they could read, poor things.

DELFINA THINKS:

At the mayor's house, a group of important people was waiting for us. Father Arcanjo proudly introduced me to each of them.

I told some of the more curious people that I had completed a course at the School of Hygiene and Public Health, that I had a past in Germany, as my family came from there. I had specialized in defective children because I was an excellent caregiver and very reliable in administering medications. I met three women, three sisters. They were introduced as the women of the big house and had taken care of a baby who had showed up by the roadside. They named the boy Lázaro, already a young man with a promising future. He said he wanted to be mayor of Santa Graça. White like me, lucky boy. The old ladies were very close to the priest and the town doctor, but they were very discreet. They rarely opened their door. They didn't even have any servants except for a black maid, Íris, who occasionally did the tougher cleaning of the yard. Lobélia, Alpínia, and Dália were interested in me. They wanted to know my story. I told them that the tragedy of my life was losing my parents, and now, alone, I was looking for a dignified occupation and a home with good, Christian people who could host me in exchange for my services.

There was no shortage of interest. The mayor himself told me about a brother who, due to God's impiety, had two feeble-minded children. One was very ill, and the other would soon get sick as well. The sister-in-law was very tired from the work, and the black maids who served the house had become very fond of the children, which caused them a lot of trouble. At night, the girl Carolina, in convulsions from the medicine, would scream the names of the black women. These black people only brought trouble. A German woman, stern and rigid, highly recommended by the priest, could only be a gift from God. It wasn't long before I was introduced to the mayor's brother. He offered me a room in their mansion in the center of Santa Graça, one of the largest in town, with gardens, peacocks, blacks, and *pardos*. The mayor insisted to Father Arcanjo that I accept the job offer. With little to decide, we agreed that I would start the next day. I would sleep that night at the parish house and head to the new house in the morning. Father Arcanjo would accompany me so I wouldn't get the address wrong.

FATHER ARCANJO COMMENTS:
Everyone has taken a liking to you, Helga.

Come, the maids have set the table for an evening snack. I taught them some refinement in the presentation of the food. They learned quickly, considering… you know. Sit at the table, come, come, the house of the Lord is your house.

FATHER ARCANJO WHISPERS:
about the sacristy;
about the Sunday lunches,
about the big house;
about the superiority of the races;
about the ambition of Santa Graça;
about the Constitution;
about the *Eugenics Journal*;
about science;
about bones;
about dentists and doctors;

about the eugenics meetings;
about not everyone having the
capacity to understand such
advancement;
about keeping this a secret;
about God above all.

HELGA COMMENTS:
Peace, Father Arcanjo.
 I am on your side, which is the right side. There are no doubts.
 I would also like to gather, have functions, get involved. I come to do good. Count on me.

DELFINA DESIRES
Raquel;
to forget Raquel.

FATHER ARCANJO LIKES
boys.

FATHER ARCANJO ANNOUNCES:
Whenever the bulletin from São Paulo arrives, I will let you know. We read it together in the meetings. The ladies of the big house, I, Dr. Lírio, Mr. Olavo. Sometimes, young Lázaro, who needs

to familiarize himself with the laws and culture. One day, that young boy will be the mayor of Santa Graça.

Each one of us is an important part of a chain that puts Santa Graça above any other town in the country in terms of eugenic science. You don't need to have dinner on the night of the meetings. The black maids cook the most divine things, God forgive me for my gluttony.

The debates are weekly, but the bulletin reaches us more sporadically. The interpretation we make of eugenic theory and science is an advanced, ambitious interpretation. We are committed to practicing what is written in a subtle and suggested manner. We have no time to waste.

We are aware of each person's task in the group. Mine is carried out without fanfare and is of great nobility:

Resemblances are favored by heredity, while differences are a mark of the environment in which the individual has lived. What a responsibility for each of us! Blessed are those who have received from their ancestors and parents' perfect health and who, thanks to them, have been able to grow and live in a healthy environment.

Your duty, therefore, is clear. What you have received, you must pass on pure, free from any stain. In this way, you will contribute to the continuation of a good race and provide valuable services to society. (*Eugenics Bulletin*, January 1929)

> It is not difficult to follow to the letter what science tells me, Helga. Above me, God and the well-being of human beings. Our intentions are noble. When we become the past, we will know that we were on the right side of history, a glorious, patriotic, and Christian side. I'm glad you are with us.
>
> **HELGA HEARS:**
> Radio Minas reports:

The police in the town of Monte Novo, in the state of Minas Gerais, apprehended an illegal human bone bank. Two *pardos* were arrested on the spot. The two men stated that they worked cleaning the remains that were sold to doctors and dentists. When sought by the police, the doctor and dentist from Monte Novo denied any involvement. The two *pardos* were taken to the municipal jail.

> **DELFINA THINKS:**
> Our task force for the improvement of the inhabitants of Santa Graça

continued without faltering. Under my care was the girl Mirtes. Due to a blood deformity, Mirtes was born blind, quite mentally impaired, and with deformed feet. Her future was harsh. She would be left without anyone to care for her, old in a wheelchair, useless, causing enormous work and high expenses to control the screams and scratches on her skin, which she herself inflicted with much persistence and depth. Her father, the mayor's brother, had a beautiful piazza built at the house so that Mirtes could enjoy the sunny days, walk a little, and scream without disturbing the neighbors. Some black maids served us when we needed juice and water or when it was necessary to carry Mirtes. Manual labor was not something within my capacities. There were others who would do this kind of thing. The piazza was large and full of echoes. The sound of Mirtes' screams causes the children in the neighborhood to have nightmares. No one knew what the girl existed for. Pushing her wheelchair around the garden, I saw my white cotton gloves.

 Die, Mirtes, die.

HELGA EXPLAINS:

I am still shaken. What a tragedy! It was on a Saturday morning, the family was out at a rally and political work. Some black maids on the property, Mirtes and I. I held tightly to the handles of the girl's wheelchair. She was very agitated. I remember perhaps forgetting to give her the medicine that calmed her, but I'm not sure. I have too many concerns and responsibilities. Something may have slipped by and I didn't notice. Mirtes was fidgeting in the chair. She bled from a deep scratch, but I believe, though I can't remember exactly, that the blood flowing was caused by the defective girl herself. Every time she scratched herself, I would scream for her to stop, and the more I screamed, the more she did it. I grabbed her arms, that thin child's skin, but I was extremely careful not to hurt her. Still, while I tried to prevent the scratches by holding her firmly, though never with force — never that! — she would make my fingers press into her fragile little body. It was she who was hurting herself, that poor girl. These children go straight to the kingdom of heaven, poor things. I brought this matter to the family's attention. Mirtes was being impossible with this habit of scratching and hurting herself. Fortunately, the family had complete trust in me, knowing it was indeed the girl torturing herself, even though it was I who stayed with her all the time, and she stained my hands with blood so many times. On the way to take a little stroll in the house's piazza, we headed toward the beautiful marble fountain built in the center of the space. I don't know exactly what happened to that girl, she suddenly got so worked up that she jumped into the fountain while I was trying to shoo away some bees that were bothering us. As always, all I ever tried to do was to protect Mirtes. We still don't know how Mirtes managed to get out of the wheelchair and jump, as if she were healthy, into the pond. Sometimes, God works miracles, that's true. What a great misfortune that the girl didn't know how to swim. She screamed, but while I was preoccupied with getting rid of the bees, I thought the screams were the usual ones, the ones of madness. Poor Mirtes, may the Lord keep her in a place of rest, was buried two days later, and I, having no further use in that home, was transferred to work at the Alencar house. I went to take care of Augusto.

DELFINA THINKS:
Die, Mirtes, Augusto, you retarded ones, die.

LÁZARO THINKS:
I want to be mayor when I grow up.
I will send all the mad people to Fazenda Horizontina.
I will build a mental asylum.
I will marry Helga. Helga is white and clean.
Íris is black and dirty.

DELFINA THINKS
just like Helga.

HELGA EXPLAINS TO THE POLICE:
I spent a lot of sad days due to the loss of our dear Mirtes. A tormented soul, surely. With so much madness within

that frail body, perhaps she would now find peace under God's care in eternity and divine mercy.

I often visited the mayor's brother's house, such good people, who received me so kindly. Despite Mirtes' death we kept a faithful friendship. In my visits I noticed that the black girls who roamed around while I took care of Mirtes had been substituted by other black girls. Not that they were much different, they were almost the same, but I noticed a couple of distinctive characteristics.

In that week I mentioned the substitution to Father Arcanjo. He assured me that everything was under God's control and that the servants probably just left, as black people always avoid work and responsibility.

After so much time in the mayor's brother's house and with the loss of our dear Mirtes, I ended up going to work at little Augusto's house. I started to really care for him. Gustinho was seven when I arrived. It was not easy, taking care of him, he kept my hands full. He was extremely mentally disabled and behaved like a baby. Sometimes, when he cried a lot I had to take him into the bedroom, lock the door and nurse him. He sucked my breasts as if there was really milk coming out of them. Even without being fed, he would calm down. (I miss Sister Raquel.) I let him play with my round breasts and he would lick and suck them. Things that only a mother would let a son do, but I cared too much for that boy! There were times where Gustinho was so difficult to deal with, that I would lock ourselves in the bedroom and force him to nurse. He tried to pull away and reject it, but I was much stronger than him and at some point he would do what calmed him down and accept that it was what was best for him. I nursed him at least once a day. He looked like an angel lying on my breasts. He sucked on hard, that boy didn't even seem sick.

His parents were not psychologically apt to take care of a little boy that was so exhausting. When he grew up a bit, I noticed that he wanted to touch my private parts. For his own good, and so that he wouldn't scream, I taught him all he needed to do. He stayed very quiet, just like a little lamb, the boy (Sister Raquel). Once there was a problem: he, who never spoke, screamed during a family lunch that I forced him to do bad things. A dagger to my heart. How could a child lie so much! Obviously, Augusto's parents didn't believe that little imbecile, but one of his aunts started looking at me funny, wouldn't let me be alone with Augusto anymore whenever he needed calming down and would follow my steps wherever I went. Augusto even invented a story with a bunch of details about me. Such nonsense. Anyways I was devastated when, one day, in the bathtub, I turned around to get a bar of soap and a pack of potassium permanganate and, as I read the instructions, Gustinho drowned himself. It all happened so fast that I couldn't really save him. I didn't sleep for months thinking of my boy, who was now a little angel on Jesus' side. May God guard his soul. I miss him a lot.

DELFINA MISSES
Sister Raquel.

FATHER ARCANJO EXPLAINS TO THE POLICE:

Santa Graça is a paradise. Nothing bad happens here. We are good people. My parish is always full, with truly Christian people. I was just as alarmed as you were by this story about the bone bank, about the murder of sick children. I ask that you respect us. Look at each of us: imagine if people like me; Miss Helga, a young woman who dedicates her life to the town's sick children; Mr. Olavo, an honest man who goes door to door selling books, an exemplary father still mourning the loss of little Ícaro; Dr. Lírio, an intellectual and a man devoted to caring for others; the three elderly sisters, who do nothing but raise a young boy who isn't even theirs—imagine if such people could be involved in something like this.

Respect us, for we have nothing to do with it. Those *pardos* you found are lying about our supposed involvement. That Mr. Jão da Lavagem, poor fellow, with a name like that, doesn't even know what he's saying. Do you really think that we would strip the skin and flesh off black people, cook them in cauldrons for lunch, and dispose of the thick fat this individual, who grew up among pigs, refers to? Oh, spare me. I pity this poor man, Jão da Lavagem. I have heard many cases of black people and *pardos* who lie a lot to try to gain some status, some social prominence. I pity him because everyone knows this man is scheming to portray good people in a bad light. God forgive me, but they are even capable of threats and blackmail. You are free men—I only hope that faith serves as the compass for your actions and that you rely on clarity to see who is who. God will deliver justice, but you must not fail to do your part. Arrest these individuals at once, for they clearly don't have God in their hearts. I ask the Lord to forgive them for casting suspicion on righteous people.

SANTA GRAÇA HEARS:
Radio Minas reports:

The police in the town of Monte Novo, in the state of Minas Gerais, have seized a clandestine bone bank containing the remains of both children and adults. Two *pardos* were caught in the act and arrested. The two individuals stated that they worked cleaning the remains, which were sold to doctors and dentists through a scheme operating in the small town of Santa Graça. The investigation aims to interrogate a priest, a doctor, three women, an encyclopedia salesman, a nurse who cares for "defective" children, and a *pardo* who collects scraps and fat from the town's homes. When approached by the police, the doctor and dentist from Monte Novo denied any involvement—both their own and that of the distinguished residents of Santa Graça. The man who collects grease and scraps has been detained and is expected to testify. The two *pardos* remain imprisoned in the municipal jail.

HELGA EXPLAINS TO THE POLICE:
After Gustinho passed away, I spent a month at the parish house, recovering from the devastating loss that was that angel's death. Amongst all that grief, the priest told me that there was a house where they would soon need me. The house right next to the big house where the three elderly women live. The boy was Ícaro, and his father was the town's encyclopedia salesman.

As soon as they called me, I pulled myself together and started my new job. At least I never lacked work in such a lovely town as Santa Graça.

Of course, I noticed that grimy-colored man passing by daily with cans of thick grease. God forbid, it even looked like human fat, it was so dense. I have no idea where he got that from, but I'd swear it wasn't from the center of Santa Graça—because here, we are good people. God save me from such horror. What a shame that a man of such ilk would stain the honor of a town like this!

DR. LÍRIO EXPLAINS TO THE POLICE:

The map of Santa Graça is transforming as our success spreads and becomes a reality. But we have an issue. Mata Cavalo is the area of town where the poor and black people live. They build mud shacks and come down from their hills every day to work in the town's homes.

That man who raised our suspicions, that Jão da Lavagem—just listen to that name—is a desolate soul who cannot read, talks to pigs, and lives in Mata Cavalo. The poor man's house is a pigsty. They say he lives alongside the very swine he slaughters for a few coins from the butcher. I treated him when he was still a boy. But coming from Mata Cavalo, he had little chance of becoming somebody. The word around town is that he has grown envious and deceitful. As a doctor, however, I can assure you that this damned soul is suffering from some mental delusions. It is quite common in certain races. If he does not stop causing all this unrest among the people of Santa Graça, perhaps I should speak with some colleagues—doctors of the highest standing—to have him evaluated. There are excellent mental asylums in the region. It would cost us nothing to help such a man, who is clearly in a state of despair and mental incoherence.

But you gentlemen are wise and have sound judgment. I trust you will do the right thing.

ÍRIS THINKS:

Jão doesn't lie, he never has. If I say what I saw, they'll kill me, and I need to take care of mother. I'll ask for a confession with Father Arcanjo.

I will never forget that appendicitis outbreak in town. That was strange. If I hadn't had the surgery, I could have Joaquim here, alive with me.

By now, little Ícaro has already arrived in Japan. Poor soul. Dona Rosa might as well die. Die, old woman, die.

LÁZARO SAYS TO JÃO DA LAVAGEM:

Íris doesn't wash her dirty hand. Íris' hand is black.

I'm going to be mayor when I grow up.

DELFINA THINKS:

Íris is yet another resident of Mata Cavalo who needs to stay among us. Still the black woman gives us some trouble. She must be closely watched. We can't quite figure out which side the miserable woman is on. She never says anything, always silent, always mute. She was stubborn about having children when she dated and, in fact, almost got engaged to that fool Jão da Lavagem, who now lies to the police. Her black womb wouldn't accept children, though. One day, the poor thing had appendicitis, and Dr. Lírio took care of everything, operating on her in the town hospital, full of white people. After that, she gave up her obsession with bringing more black babies into the world. In any case, Íris works for us and does everything more or less as instructed.

Well, all I know is that the future has arrived. The science of eugenics already gives us the foundation to ensure we're not distracted by any social or racial claims. Black people had their chance. They were freed, emancipated. And what did they do? Nothing, as always. They've only ever worked when threatened or punished. A lazy kind of people who aspire to be like white society but never do what it takes. Today, we know this. We know that each race has its place in society. It has always been this way, and despite some minor revolutions, the future has arrived, and now black people know their place. They even started using the term "racism." What about the racism they have against me? No one seems to notice that. Or do they think I don't see the looks they give me, the whispers among themselves when I complain that there's not enough sugar in the juice or that the coffee is poorly brewed? Do they think I don't notice the difference in how they treat each other compared to how they treat me? They are mistaken. If there is racism here, there is racism there, too. Even so, they are useful. They have strong teeth, and through them, we gather genetic information that can help us create the super-race our country deserves, starting with Santa Graça. Imagine if every person had the healthy teeth of a black person? Their bones are valuable. But we have no use for their skin.

Íris is quite useful, and I believe that's the only reason the Santa Graça eugenics council hasn't suggested her permanent removal from the town. Who else would scrub the floors with the brute strength of that black woman? They serve us, the unfortunate ones. But perhaps not for much longer. Even though I prefer to keep my distance from Íris, she must be kept close. Father Arcanjo, who hears her confessions, tells us we must keep her very near.

DELFINA LOCKS
the door.

DELFINA SPREADS
her legs.

DELFINA MISSES
Raquel.

HELGA TELLS THE POLICE:
The black maid, Íris, opened the gate, and I was received by the sick boy's mother and grandmother.

I listened to their concerns. One of which was the growing closeness and attachment between Ícaro and Íris. The two would talk and sometimes even laugh together. It was all very scandalous. The grandmother, Dona Rosa, also told me that she had, on occasion, found in the trash or inside Íris's bag, medicines and pills that Ícaro should have taken. That black maid had the audacity to withhold them and even defied the household's authority, claiming that the medication made the boy worse, that it locked his mouth, made him drool, and even caused hallucinations. Obviously, that woman knew nothing about medicine or health, as she had never studied or understood science.

We were simply following what we had read, and precisely for that reason, there were no counterarguments— because we were protected by what scholars and intellectuals had told us. Poor black people. And now they are lying about us again. They know they are wrong, but we know the truth.

That lost soul, the man who collects *lavagem*, does not seem to be in his right mind. I have already spoken to Dr. Lírio – we must take care of him. These people attack us, but we are here to help them, even if they often do not deserve it. Gentlemen, please be aware of this man's mistakes. We expect an apology from you later. You have caused us enough trouble already. Even the holy priest is being accused. May God forgive you.

ÍRIS MISSES
Ícaro;
Joaquim;
Íris wants to kill Helga;
Die, blondie, die.

HELGA EXPLAINS TO THE POLICE:

During our conversation, I assured the two women of the house that Ícaro would receive the best treatment from me. He would take all his medicine religiously, and when God willed it, He would take him to rest like an angel. After all, Ícaro deserved nothing less than to become an angel, after such a difficult life, despite his young age.

DELFINA THINKS:

I observed the house. It had two floors, with a long staircase cutting through the middle. At the entrance, a sidewalk in need of repair, with loose and uneven stones. My room was next to the boy's. A bathroom to be shared with him. A large bathtub so that Ícaro could swim whenever he wanted. In the living room, a balcony and a veranda overlooking the backyard of the three elderly sisters and Lázaro. I paused for a moment and saw the boy playing with his bones. He saw me. I smiled and waved. We were all friends in Santa Graça, a truly lovely place. One day Lázaro will become mayor.

LÁZARO SHOUTS

Helga, will you marry me?

Helga, when I grow up, I will be mayor, and I will lock all the retarded people up at Fazenda Horizontina, except for Íris, because Íris is black and dirty.

Jão da Lavagem is stupid because he pulls a cart.

HELGA EXPLAINS TO THE POLICE:

Despite the various dangers in the house, I would do the most impeccable of jobs, which was to take care of yet another defective child from Santa Graça. Now, I just had to hope that, unlike my other children, Ícaro would be luckier and wouldn't get involved in any accidents.

When I saw the door slightly open to Ícaro's room, I saw that the boy was curled up on the bed. Íris was telling him not to worry. She was calling him to go see the ducks from the window, to see Lázaro playing, "that crazy boy," I heard that irresponsible woman say.

The boy's mother gave me the freedom to start my task right then.

I stopped at the door and watched Íris help Ícaro get up to distract him by the window. He was afraid of me. Can you imagine being afraid of me, a person who lives to take care of children that everyone else despises, everyone rejects? One day, they'll give me a medal, that's for sure. The black maid held the boy in her arms in an extremely intimate fashion, a scandal. God forbid I even think the worst, holding him so closely like that. God forgive me.

DELFINA REMEMBERS:
Ícaro looked at me terrified, drooling and crying. Íris was caressing his hair. She dragged a chair with one of her feet and placed the boy on it to see the backyard of the big house. "Look, Ícaro, how the sun is shining today. There's going to be a rainbow in the water, let's wait and watch." She spoke to him with such affection, and she looked at me with anger. Racist! "Look at Lázaro playing with the bones, can you see, Ícaro? In two minutes, the sun will shine so strongly on the water in the ducks' tank that we'll see it shine like the other side of the world shines, over in Japan."

HELGA EXPLAINS TO THE POLICE:

I approached to see what they could see from the window. There was a tank where ducks swam and drank water that was muddy and smelled awful. It was right under the boy's room window. Íris ordered me to move away because he was afraid. I didn't budge because I never take orders from black people. That infuriated me, that audacity. I grabbed those clumps of the black woman's curly hair as she held the boy firmly, with half his body outside the window. I'm sure you would agree with me.

DELFINA REMEMBERS:

Of course, Íris wasn't going to let Ícaro fall. She was very attached to that boy. I know I pulled her hair, grabbed her skin with force and intention to reach the bone. I know that woman, despite her color, wouldn't have done anything bad to that sick child. If Ícaro fell, it was by accident… Her anger was directed at me. Such a racist!

HELGA EXPLAINS TO THE POLICE:

If the boy Ícaro fell, maybe it's because Íris didn't hold him tight enough, or maybe the little boy just got tired of living such a difficult life and finally had the good sense to throw himself into the infinite that would reach the other side of the world. I didn't even need to work in the house. Things were resolved on their own. He flew, the boy Ícaro, just like it happened in mythology.

Íris, that poor soul fled to Horizontina after the accident – the farm that holds the ghost of Gregório without Skin.

This is all I have to say about the boy Ícaro. Gentlemen, please consider this case closed. I am very tired of this conversation and have already cooperated with everything I can. Now, you must excuse me because it is my duty to assist Dr. Lírio. We do not stop working for the good of Santa Graça. Let's take care of the man who attacks us with delusions, that Jão. And here you are, interrogating those who do good. The world is truly upside down.

Gregório without Skin

LÁZARO SHOUTS:
Íris, you let that retarded Ícaro fall. The police will get you. Your hand is black, dirty, it slips.

ÍRIS LISTENS TO
Radio Minas;
the bone bank;
children and adults;
doctors and dentists;
pardos and individuals;
arrested.

ÍRIS EXPLAINS TO THE POLICE:
I started to arrange my work at Mr. Olavo's and Mrs. Ondina's house with that of the old women in the big house, because they weren't that far from one another. On Fridays, when I finished earlier at Ícaro's house, I would go to the big house to wash the yard. Friday was the day to kill the animals for cooking. Every Sunday, without fail, the old women would cook meat that took until the following Sunday to become tender, when it was served to Father Arcanjo. They would leave me a lunchbox, but I made a point of throwing it away. Their cooking disgusted me. I can't explain it, but I felt repulsed by it.

They barely spoke, barely went out; strange. They

spoiled Lázaro when he was a boy, and now they spoil him as he's grown. They planted the idea in his head that he will be the mayor of Santa Graça. Soon, the boy will think he wants to be president of the country.

One Friday, after I had washed and scrubbed the bloodstained floor of the courtyard of the big house, I set aside some *lavagem* for Jão, who used to be my love. After we lost Joaquim and tried for another child with no luck, Jão gave up on me. He went looking for a mother for his children and ended up falling for Maria das Graças, also from Mata Cavalo. Whenever I had to find him and give him the *lavagem*, I felt my stomach tighten with love. I never forgot him or Joaquim, whom he put inside me. Jão left me, but he's not a liar, no. He's a good man.

ÍRIS THINKS:

One Friday, while I waited for Jão to come by and pick up *lavagem* from the big house of the three old women, the lazy Lázaro came shouting and grabbing the hem of my skirt. He said he needed to get a piece of the puzzle that was missing to finish assembling the bird-man and that he was afraid to go alone to the second floor. I told the boy I wasn't allowed up there. I told Lázaro to go look for the old women, but two of them had gone to the market and the third was in the woods slaughtering animals to cook the meat. I told the little brat to have patience and wait until one of them returned, but he couldn't wait.

I said there was no way to go up because it was locked with seven keys and I didn't know where anything was kept.

Lázaro ran off and came back out of breath, handing me a bunch of three keys, one for each old woman. My hands almost burned.

It's true I risked a lot with those keys and with each step I took. The old women could appear at any moment.

But none of them appeared, and I discovered what was kept in that part of the house. Lázaro told me that all I had to do was open the door, and he would run to get the missing piece. That's exactly what happened, and that fraction of time was enough to terrify me even beyond death. With the creak of the door opening, my eyes opened wide, and there they were, gagged, so thin that you could see their bones, the little black boys, whose muffled screams could be heard every now and then. Ícaro wasn't crazy: the attic was indeed haunted. There were little black boys gagged and wasting away. Their bright eyes full of utter despair met mine. Many of the boys were the children of the black women from Mata Cavalo.

The old women arrived and followed their routine as usual. I looked deep into the eyes of those three old women and couldn't believe such wickedness. I knew about the plan to bleach us, the entire town, but I had never seen a little black boy disappearing up close.

Did I hear or not hear Lázaro tell Jão that the fat from the house was human fat? I kept thinking about that, but I think Dr. Lírio is right: I've been tired, needing to rest my head, which has been playing tricks on me. Lázaro is a liar. A bad boy indeed. A devilish spirit. That thing will never become human, even if it becomes mayor.

ÍRIS CONFESSES:

Father Arcanjo, you relieve me, by the love of Our Lady. I discovered where the boys who disappeared are. Father Arcanjo, I don't want to know, but I do know. You relieve me, by the love of the Holy Spirit, I can't bear such a tormenting secret. What do they do with those little black boys, Father Arcanjo? Why didn't they have teeth? Father Arcanjo, help me.

Father, I think I heard Lázaro tell Jão what's in those cans of fat. I've been nervous about this, feeling sick with disgust. But Lázaro is a little liar, isn't he, Father?

> **FATHER ARCANJO COMMENTS**
> with Dr. Lírio;
> with Olavo;
> with the three old women;
> with Helga;
> with Lázaro;
> that Íris knows.

> **ÍRIS PRAYED**
> all night;
> The Our Father;
> the Hail Mary;
> out of fear.

> **DR. LÍRIO ANNOUNCES:**
> Ms. Íris, you've been serving us with so much dedication for such a long

time. I met with Father Arcanjo and some other prominent citizens of Santa Graça, and we decided that you deserve some rest. Please inform your greatly respected mother that you are moving. You'll have a large house just for you, and nothing will be lacking. Even Father Arcanjo will visit you weekly to hear your confessions. There have been many events in this town lately. We need to put the house in order, and you are important to Santa Graça. Our wish is for you to have good health. Have you ever taken time off to rest?

Everything is ready for you to take possession of Fazenda Horizontina.

We would like you to accept our humble gift. Of course, Ms. Íris, you deserve much more, but it's all we have for now. Please accept our honest offer.

ÍRIS GETS

a farm;
new clothes;
two horses;
servants;
plenty;
a headache.

ÍRIS GIVES

her silence.

ÍRIS EXPLAINS TO THE POLICE

the priest;
the doctor;
the old women;
the father of the family;
the nurse;
the boy Lázaro;
are all good citizens.
I'm a witness.

ÍRIS GETS

a farm;
new clothes;
servants;
horses;
a headache.

ÍRIS GIVES

her silence.

ÍRIS THOUGHT

I, Íris, a black woman from Mata Cavalo, will be the owner of Fazenda Horizontina.
I'll have servants.
I'll have horses.

It's a shame to leave my Joaquim buried far from me.

Horizontina has existed since 1815.

It was built to shelter a rich Portuguese family who arrived in the region to plant coffee. Over time, they also ventured into cattle farming and took control of everything. A farm as far as the eye could see, with a master's house made of tabatinga (a type of wood), a chapel, slave quarters, a slaughterhouse, a pond, coffee plantations, pasture, and smaller houses for the foreman, priest, and workers who were neither black nor white. The peace in Horizontina ended when a slave named Gregório got into a fight with a captain of the woods and refused to do cart-pulling work because he claimed he was an artist. Gregório would spend his mornings painting arabesques on the friezes at the master's request and to his missus's liking. He took great care in it, drawing, with precision, guaxes, chestnut-bellied seed-finches, and all kinds of gaturamo: king, with a large beak, and niggling. He would carve pineapples, papayas, orange-limes in plaster. It took time because he did it meticulously. It is said that on one occasion, Gregório was about to finish a drawing when the foreman entered the hall, kicked the black man, and with a whip in hand, ordered him to pull the cart to bring the priest, since the missus needed to confess. Gregório refused, saying that cart-pulling was a job for animals and that he even knew how to draw. The foreman grabbed Gregório by the hair and dragged him to the slaughterhouse. Gregório spat on the foreman and scratched him all over. With blood in his eyes, out of hate for the black man, the foreman first plunged a machete into Gregório's belly, then horizontally slits his throat. He shoved his hand into the black man's neck and pulled out his still-beating heart. Wild animals gathered around, and the foreman threw the bloodied organ to the pigs to eat. In less than five minutes, Gregório had neither a heart nor a life. Not satisfied with the carnage, the foreman made a cut in Gregório's skin and peeled off all his leather, slicing the man's body into fillets that were later fed to the dogs. Gregório's skin was left to dry out to serve as an example to the other slaves. All that remained of the disobedient black man was his dental arch, which the pigs rejected, but it ended up being used by the foreman, who had each of the teeth embedded in his cherished hunting rifle, decorated with emeralds and diamonds. The very same rifle that, years later, killed its own master at the hands of his wife, who caught her husband in an affair with a black woman in the banana grove of the farm. Since the day of Gregório's death, Horizontina has been haunted by the black man's spirit, lingering around the master's house. The slave had a daughter who was sent, along with her mother, through an exchange transaction to a farm in the Catete region, in Rio de Janeiro. The man's spirit never left. The Portuguese family lived in fear because the children would cry and tremble with terror at the sight of Gregório without Skin walking around the house at night, through rooms that he had painted himself. It didn't matter how much the older folks explained that he was a black slave who didn't mean anything. The children didn't see a black man, they saw a man without skin, with his flesh peeled off, floating between rooms and haunting the entire night. The darker the night, the more Gregório could be seen. Out of fear, once a child ran out of their room in the middle of the night and threw themselves into the pond. They died, they said, by Gregório's command, the man without skin. The family fled Horizontina and moved to Bahia because there were too many ghosts in Minas.

Since then, only wandering souls live in Horizontina. Now, Íris is the owner of everything.

ÍRIS WEEPS:

Life in Horizontina is always the same. Sometimes Father Arcanjo comes, but he hasn't been around lately. I've been wishing for Dona Rosa to go to hell. Every morning, a truck brings some men to ask me if everything is okay. They say they're asking on the part of Dr. Lírio and Helga.

I've been so lonely in this vast land. I miss Joaquim and even Jão, who hasn't been mine for a long time.

I wanted to go see the town. Just for one day. If I left, no one would even notice.

I told my mother I wouldn't be long. Poor thing; she was dying more and more every day.

I threw my things in a bag and hid in the back of the men's truck, which was about to return the eleven kilometers to Santa Graça. When the engine was about to start, they found me. I begged them to keep it a secret, and I promised I'd confess to Father Arcanjo once I arrived at the parish house. I explained that I was the owner of the farm, but it didn't matter, they were going to talk to Dr. Lírio and that horrible Helga.

When the truck arrived at Santa Graça, I asked to be let off at the entrance and ended up going around the back of Pirapetinga to reach the other side of Mata Cavalo. It had been so long since I'd gone up that hill lined with banana and mango trees, the smell of home. One that I so deeply missed.

From afar, I saw Ester and Carolina washing clothes. I

had been missing them. When they saw me, they grabbed the clothes, crumpled them in a hurry, stuffed them in the laundry basket, and ran inside, running away from me. It was obvious. I called each of their names, but they managed to escape. I reached Joaquim's tree and thought of Jão, married, with a living child, and who had surely already forgotten our dead boy. I sat on the dirt ground, with my ear pressed to the earth, and I could hear my Quinquim's[9] heartbeat. From the window, Carolina, Marta, Tiana, and Ester watched me suspiciously. It seemed like they didn't know who I was. Soon, a crowd gathered in the cracks of the lace curtains of the houses on the street. Everyone was looking at me, but no one spoke. It felt like I had done something terribly wrong when what really happened was that I had gone to seek a better life, with more comfort. I wanted to have somewhere to die, not become what everyone becomes in Mata Cavalo. Here, we are born, we grow, and we die. No one leaves unless it's to be buried or to work in the houses of the doctors in the town center. Joaquim didn't even get to do that.

What I came here for was to dig a hole and take my baby with me. I was going to get him a big tomb in Horizontina. I would have the men build a mausoleum, a house just for my boy. I was going to ask Father Arcanjo to arrange for marble to make it beautiful. The Father knows someone who makes little angel statues. It's called sculpture. I was going to have them make a little black-faced angel with white wings, pure, to honor my Quinquim. I was going to mark his birth date with a star and on the same day, a cross to show the life he

---

9. *Quinquim* is a pet name for Joaquim.

never had the chance to live. He was born a little gray bundle, and that was it. Poor thing.

That's what I told Dr. Lírio I wanted to do during my visit to Santa Graça. I also needed to understand why Dr. Lírio, Helga, the Father, and Mr. Olavo had forgotten about me in that vast place called Horizontina. In the late afternoon, between five and six o'clock, you hear the crickets, and then nothing. A feeling of anguish. Here in Mata Cavalo, when it was nighttime, there was drumming in the yard, the noise of radios some houses had.

I knelt on the ground, dug carefully so I wouldn't hurt my dead boy, and pulled Joaquim from that orange, thick earth. I wrapped my baby in a banana leaf I found there. That could have been a baby, or a little chick, it was hard to tell. After all this time, the bundle had turned into a little brown and gray ball, and there was a dead weight in it, without a soul for many years.

Everyone had their eyes on me. Wide, fixed eyes.

Mr. Antunes didn't want to let me walk away. He said Joaquim belonged to Jão too, and that the man worked all day just to come at night and lay his palm on this pile of dirt, now all turned over.

I shouted at Mr. Antunes to leave me alone and that no one should tell a mother what to do with her child.

When I walked down from Mata Cavalo with my child wrapped up, I reached the town center and saw Dr. Lírio talking to Helga.

It was good timing because I really needed to speak to those two.

I called their names, and Dr. Lírio entered the bank, pretending not to see me.

ÍRIS SCREAMS:
I want to come back to Santa Graça, Dr. Lírio.

I don't want to stay in Horizontina anymore.

There are ghosts of slaves there, did you know?

It's crickets in the afternoon and ghosts all night long, did you know?

If you knew that, I doubt you would have taken me and my mother to live there, because you're a good man.

Since little Ícaro left for Japan, I haven't slept, my soul can't find peace.

Since Lázaro made me open the door to the little black boys, my heart hasn't calmed down. Dr. Lírio, look at what I brought: Joaquim, the one you took from me. You said it was appendicitis, but it was my Quinquim, Dr. Lírio, such a pity.

HELGA, DR. LÍRIO, OLAVO, DONA ONDINA, DONA ROSA, LÁZARO, THE THREE OLD WOMEN, AND THE WHOLE TOWN LOOK
at Íris with disbelief, not saying a word, as the police tie her hands, making Joaquim fall, roll on the ground, and into the ditch that drained the rain.

ÍRIS LOSES
her mind;
her Quinquim again.

ÍRIS SCREAMS:
But, Dr. Lírio, the horse has already left the barn. There's nobody, nothing is left. You told me nothing would be lacking. I want to build a mausoleum for my boy, will you help? I need to pay the men to build the little house for the dead, and I want a little angel with a black face and white wings right at the entrance of the tomb. A little star marking that Quinquim left my womb on October 18th, 1929, and died on October 18th, 1929. It's even funny. Same day, same year. Poor thing. A little angel with a black face.

But the wings, I want them white, pure.

You haven't stopped by anymore.

The Father said he would return with supplies, but my mother and I don't even have soap anymore. I want to go back, Dr. Lírio, I'm so lonely there. You, Helga, the old women, Mr. Olavo, you all can rest easy, our secret is well kept.

I didn't even need Horizontina to keep our secret. You didn't have to do all that.

SANTA GRAÇA SEES
the police taking Íris, who was causing
a commotion, back to Horizontina.

IN HORIZONTINA,
THE NIGHT FALLS:
A cart stops. A truck parks.

Father Arcanjo, the three old women, Helga, Lázaro, Olavo, and Dr. Lírio enter the master house.

Íris, with tearful eyes, seemed to have been waiting for them. Sitting in the rocking chair in the entrance hall, she could still hear the crickets.

She invites the guests inside.
Close your eyes, Íris.

ÍRIS CLOSES HER EYES.
When she opens them again, Joaquim, Ícaro, the sick children from Santa Graça, and the little black boys from Mata Cavalo are in front of her. She also sees her mother and Gregório, who wore his black skin.

First Readers

Jessica Dettrick (1) AUSTRALIA

Morgan deBoer (1) USA

Alyssa Reeder (1) USA

Eva Hu (1) USA

Rachel Lauren Myers (1) USA

Heather Colley (2) ENGLAND

Sean Callahan (1) USA

Maria Diment (1) USA

Jamie Blundell (1) ENGLAND

Mickey Meixner (1) GERMANY

Benjamin Beck (1) GERMANY

Randal Greene (1) USA

Jeremy Wallace (1) USA

Yasaman Moghadamnia (1) USA

Jake Pusey (1) USA

Melanie Talbot-Weiss (1) ENGLAND

Nathan Hallam (3) ENGLAND

Aida Greaney-Boles (1) ENGLAND

Frank Beninato (1) USA

Sophie Simonelli (1) FRANCE

Makana Eyre (1) USA

Ana Carvalho (1) BRAZIL

Brian Zielenski (1) TAIWAN

Dakota Smith (1) USA